TRAPPED IN A VIDEO GAME

ROBOTS REVOLT

Dustin Brady

Illustrations by Jesse Brady

Andrews McMeel
PUBLISHING®

Andrews McMeel Publishing
a division of Andrews McMeel Universal
1130 Walnut Street, Kansas City, Missouri 64106

www.andrewsmcmeel.com

18 19 20 21 22 SDB 10 9 8 7 6 5 4 3 2 1

ISBN Paperback: 978-1-4494-9515-2
ISBN Hardback: 978-1-4494-9623-4

Library of Congress Control Number: 2018932210

Made by:
Shenzhen Donnelley Printing Company Ltd.
Address and location of manufacturer:
No. 47, Wuhe Nan Road, Bantian Ind. Zone,
Shenzhen China, 518129
1st Printing—6/11/18

Acknowledgments

Special thanks to Jesse Brady for the cover and interior illustrations. You can check out more of Jesse's sweet artwork at jessebradyart.com.

Other Books by Dustin Brady

Trapped in a Video Game: The Invisible Invasion

Trapped in a Video Game

Superhero for a Day: The Magic Magic Eight Ball

Who Stole Mr. T?: Leila and Nugget Mystery #1

The Case with No Clues: Leila and Nugget Mystery #2

Bark at the Park: Leila and Nugget Mystery #3

Contents

PREFACE
In Case You Missed It

Stop.

Do not read another word of this book until you've finished the first two *Trapped in a Video Game* books. Seriously. Don't do it. Throw this book in a trash can if the temptation gets too strong.

"But what if I can't get those books?!" you might be asking. Great question. And if you were as good at using Amazon.com as you are at asking questions, then you'd have the first two *Trapped in a Video Game* books by now. "But I'm on a submarine, and Amazon doesn't yet deliver to submarines. Am I sunk?" You are not sunk. (Also, nice pun.) Your best bet is to request a transfer to a submarine equipped with all of the *Trapped in a Video Game* books. In the highly, HIGHLY unlikely event that your request gets denied, you may catch up by reading the following summary of the first two books. Again, this summary is only for submarine-bound readers who've already submitted a transfer request and preferably two appeals. If that's not you—trash can.

The *Trapped in a Video Game* series tells the story of Jesse Rigsby, a sixth-grader who gets—you'll never believe this—trapped in video games. His first adventure takes place inside a shooter called *Full Blast*, where he joins his friend Eric Conrad to battle man-sized praying mantises, angry sand monsters, and a super-creepy alien known as the Hindenburg. Halfway through the game, they run into Mark Whitman, a kid from their class who's been missing from the real world for nearly a month. Turns out, he's been trapped inside of *Full Blast* the whole time. Mark helps the duo escape by sacrificing himself and staying behind.

In *Trapped in a Video Game: The Invisible Invasion*, Jesse gets a chance to rescue Mark by sneaking into the video game company Bionosoft through *Go Wild*, a mobile game kind of like *Pokémon Go*. After surviving attacks by a Bigfoot, a velociraptor, and a few hundred vicious fur balls, Jesse learns that Bionosoft is trapping kids like Mark in their games on purpose to test some scary new technology. With the help of Eric and former Bionosoft employee Mr. Gregory, Jesse fights his way to the company's basement, where Mark is being held inside of a computer. The good news is that they're able to pull Mark out of his video game before it's too late. The bad news is that they have to break the system to do so, which releases everything else from Bionosoft's computers into the real world. That includes kids, weapons, and thousands upon thousands of video game bad guys.

OK, that's it. You're all caught up now. Happy submarining.

CHAPTER 1

Mayhem

EEEEEEEEEEEEEE.

The vibrating in my chest grew as the sound got louder.

EEEEEEEEEEEEEE.

It almost felt like a volcano could erupt from my chest at any second. Do you know that feeling? It's not a good feeling.

EEEEEEEEEEEEEE.

Of course, the noise wasn't even the problem. The problem was the cause of the noise—hundreds of six-foot-tall computer towers all malfunctioning at the same time, spitting out video game bad guys at an alarming rate.

EEEEEEEEEEEEEE.

Human-sized praying mantis aliens. Dinosaurs. Slime blobs. What looked like a flame-throwing robot dragon.

EEEEEEEEEEEEEE.

All of them seemed a little confused and a lot angry about getting transported from the comfort of their fake video game worlds to the very real, very loud basement of an evil video game corporation. I covered my ears, backed against a computer, and yelled for the only person who could do something. “MR. GREGORY! DO SOMETHING!”

Mr. Gregory kind of caused this whole mess in the first place by inventing a way to put people into video games, then breaking everything to get our friend Mark out of one. An arm cannon hit me in the chest just as a praying mantis noticed me.

“Here!” Mr. Gregory said without looking up from his laptop. “Hold them off while I try to turn off the power!”

Before I could remind Mr. Gregory about my poor aiming skills, the praying mantis screeched and leaped at me. I jammed my arm into the cannon, fell backward, and blasted up in the air.

“SCREECH!”

The mantis disappeared in a flash of light. I sat up and looked around me. Mayhem. Absolute mayhem.

3

After getting over the initial shock of transporting into the real world, the video game characters started doing what they do best—destroying everything in sight. To my right, a rhino with a long sword-horn was impaling computer towers over and over. To my left, two slimy swamp things fought each other. And straight ahead, five oversized cockroaches were circling something. The circle parted just long enough for me to see what they'd trapped.

"ERIC!" I yelled. My best friend, Eric Conrad, was huddled on the ground, kicking his legs wildly. I got up and blasted five times, missing horribly each time. "HEY!" I blasted again and finally hit one. They all turned at once. I blasted again. That may have been a mistake, because as soon as I did, they all flew directly at me.

"AHHHH!" *BLAST BLAST BLAST.* "AHHHH!" *BLAST BLAST—*

One of the cockroaches batted away my blaster, and then they all started circling and chattering. I tried raising my arms and yelling like you're supposed to do when you see a bear, but all that did was make them close in tighter and chatter angrier because cockroaches are not bears. One of them began feeling me with its long, creepy antennae. This was it—I was going to be eaten alive by a giant cockroach in the basement of a video game company. My parents would be so confused.

ZAP!

The cockroach feeling me with its antennae suddenly disappeared. All of the others looked up. Before they could do anything—*ZAP! ZAP! ZAP!*—they all disappeared, too. Eric stood in front of me, holding what looked like the scepter thing Loki has in *The Avengers*—only it was super high tech, so maybe if Loki was a robot, I guess?

“This just popped out of that computer over there!” Eric yelled. “I’m gonna take it home!”

“Where’s Mark?!” I asked.

“What?!”

I got right in Eric’s ear. “WHERE’S MARK?!” The *EEEEE* sound had gotten so loud that it was almost impossible to hear anything that wasn’t shouted directly into your ear.

Eric shrugged. Then his eyes got real big, and he pointed over my shoulder.

There was Mark, underneath a pile of fur balls from *Go Wild.* For every one he threw off, two more would jump on. Eric aimed his scepter and started zapping fur balls off the pile. After four or five, Mark was able to squirm out and take off. Eric and I ran after him. “We’re coming!” I shouted.

Mark turned around and yelled something, but I couldn’t make it out because of all the noise. He put his head down and sprinted as hard as he could through the computer towers. After 20 seconds of sprinting, Eric had fallen behind, but the fur balls and I were gaining on Mark. Suddenly, Mark threw a small metal ball over his shoulder. I slowed down. What was—

BOOM!

All of the fur balls disappeared in a blinding flash, and I fell onto my back so hard that the wind got knocked out of me. For a second, everything was quiet. Then the ringing started. Mark ran to me and started talking, but I couldn’t hear anything over the ringing in my ears. Finally, he leaned in real close and screamed, “SUPER GRENADE! I’M SO SORRY!”

I nodded to let Mark know I was OK, then gasped. Behind Mark was a group of 10 kids who’d also been trapped in video games. They were gathered in a semicircle to watch a battle between Eric and a giant walking robot. Eric kept trying to zap the robot with his scepter, and the robot kept rolling away. After the third unsuccessful zap, the robot smacked the scepter out of Eric's hand and picked him up.

"NO!" I ran to help my friend. Right before I could pick up the scepter, the robot snatched me, too. It lifted both of us up to its face, looked us over for a second, and then rolled back its helmet to reveal a girl with a blond ponytail at the controls.

"STOP TRYING TO KILL ME!" she yelled in a British-ish accent. Eric and I just stared with our mouths open. She could see that we were scared, so she tried a different approach.

"I'm Sam," she said.

"Eric."

"Jesse."

"Now please stop trying to kill me."

Eric gave her a thumbs-up, and she set us down. As soon as we touched the ground, Mark motioned us over to help a group of kids cornered by a pack of Starmanders. Eric grabbed his scepter and ran over.

"Hey!" I said before Sam lowered her helmet again. "Can you help us clear a path to the exit?"

Sam grinned, excited about her new job. "No worries!"

POW!

Before Sam could put her helmet back down, a sand monster the size of a house appeared behind her, wound up, and punched her robot as hard as it could. She went flying across the room.

"ROOOAARRRRRRR!"

The sand monster beat its chest like King Kong and started walking toward the Starmander battle. I frantically looked around for something to stop it.

There, behind a nearby computer tower, lay another *Full Blast* arm cannon. I rolled over, clipped it onto my left arm, and started charging.

"Come on, come on, come on," I said. I felt the *THUD-THUD-THUD* of the sand monster's lumbering and peeked out from behind the tower just in time to see him grab a particularly small kid. I looked back to see that my cannon was glowing white, telling me it'd reached full blast. Without hesitating, I rolled out from behind the computer and blasted a hole right through the sand monster's chest.

The monster looked down at the hole, then at the kid in his hand, then finally at me. It growled and flexed. The hole started closing up. The monster kept growling and flexing until it had totally healed itself. Then it threw aside the kid and started running at me.

CHAPTER 2
Robot Girl

POW!

Right before the sand monster could reach me, Sam's robot knocked it into next week with its giant fist.

Sam opened the helmet. "Get out of here!"

I scrambled away as the sand monster came back, angrier than ever. It wound up and took a swing at the robot that could have knocked down a building. Sam somehow dodged the punch and countered with a blow to the monster's stomach. The hit made the monster stumble backward a little bit, but it also swallowed up the fist in sand. Sam tried to pull the robot's fist back out, but all that did was topple the sand monster over on top of her. As the two wrestled on the ground, I ran back to Mr. Gregory, who was still sweating and typing on his laptop.

"Mr. Gregory, how can we help her?!"

He shook his head. “At least she’s got robot armor to protect her,” he said. “Look.” He pointed to his screen. Hundreds, maybe thousands, of red dots had begun surrounding pockets of green dots. “These green dots are kids, and they don’t have any protection. I need you and Eric to keep them safe until I can shut off the power and get the door open. Use anything you can get your hands on.”

I nodded, blasted a cockroach that was sneaking up on the left, and jumped onto a floating snowboard-looking thing that had just popped out of a computer. “How about thi—whoa! WHOA!”

The board took off on its own. The only other time I’d ever stepped onto a snowboard was when Eric’s cousin Evan had brought one to our sledding hill two years ago. “Hop on,” Evan had said. “It’s easy.” Snowboarding down the hill, I discovered, was surprisingly easy. Stopping was not. When I reached roughly the speed of a bullet train, I panicked, toppled over, and used my face as a brake. I hadn’t approached a snowboard since.

I flailed as I picked up steam. “ERIC!” I yelled as I passed him. “HELP!”

“Whoa!” Eric said. “Where did you get that?!”

"JUST HELP BEFORE I CRASH!" I circled again, doing my best to dodge bad guys and computers.

Eric tossed me something. "Use this!"

A jet pack. Great, so now instead of an out-of-control torpedo, I was about to become an out-of-control *flying* torpedo. I strapped on the jet pack and lifted off. Once I made it above the maze of computers, I could see that the bad guys had begun forming mobs with other creatures they knew. To my right were the aliens from *Full Blast.* The *Go Wild* creatures had teamed up on the left. Up ahead were robots and go-kart races and ghosts—and towering over everything, still trading punches, were Sam and the sand monster.

"Sam!" I yelled as I zoomed toward the battle. By now, Sam's robot had parts hanging off of it and wobbled when it walked. I zoomed in just as the sand monster raised both of its fists to deliver one final blow. "HEY!" I yelled while flying under the monster's armpits. The monster roared and turned its attention to me. I flew around and around while the monster swatted. As I circled the monster, I heard a crackling sound and smelled something burning. I looked down to see that I was flying so close that I was cooking him with the flame from my jet pack. The sand around his chest had turned black, and he was having trouble moving. Then, just as I was feeling pretty good about myself—

SMACK!

I ran right into one of the sand monster's hands. It closed around me and pulled me toward its mouth. I flailed and screamed until—

POW!

Sam's robot punched the sand monster in its brittle, jet pack–baked chest, which was enough to finally disintegrate it. The monster fell backward and dropped me into a pile of sand.

"Thanks heaps!" Sam said.

"No, thank YOU!"

That's when we heard a chorus of screams to our left. "Got it," Sam said.

Just then, another voice called out to our right. "HELP!"

"Got it," I said.

Sam nodded, grabbed me with her robot hand, and tossed me toward the scream. I flew across the battlefield until I found the source of the noise—a kid surrounded by a river of tiny robot ants. I turned off the jet pack and rode toward the kid on my hoverboard. “Hop on!” I yelled.

He grabbed me and swung onto the board just as the robot ants started climbing his pant leg. “Thank you!” he said as he brushed off the pests. I wanted to tell him that maybe he should hold off on his thanks because he might have been safer with the ants than with the world’s wobbliest hoverboard operator, but I chose to nod instead. It took all my concentration to stay upright as I looked for a safe place to stop, which is why I never even saw the blast that *ZIIING*ed right by my face.

"WHOA!" *ZIIING!* Another blast fired past me on the left side. I looked up to see that I was staring down the barrel of a robot turret machine gun. I pulled back and fell down in the middle of the aisle right on top of the kid I'd saved.

RATATATATAT.

The turret continued blasting away, but we were protected by the hoverboard still strapped to my feet. Since I'd fallen straight back, the hoverboard stuck up in the air like a shield. During a pause in the *RATATAT*, I leaned left and took a shot with my arm cannon. Miss. *RATATATATAT.* Pause. Another blast. Another miss. That's when the hoverboard disappeared and reappeared.

Uh-oh.

Based on previous experience with jet packs, I knew that the hoverboard would blink a few more times before disappearing for good.

RATATATATAT.

This would probably be my last shot. I charged up the arm cannon while counting one-Mississippi, two-Mississippi to time the next blink. When I got to three-Mississippi, I fired straight ahead. As soon as the shot left my blaster, the hoverboard disappeared, giving the blast a straight line to the turret. The shot hit its target, and the turret fizzled, popped, and pooped out.

"That was awesome!" the kid behind me said while holding up his hand for a high five. I didn't have time to return the high five because I heard another voice.

"HELP!"

It was a familiar voice. "JESSE! MARK! ROBOT GIRL! ANYONE, HELP!"

It was Eric.

I lifted off with the jet pack and took off toward the voice. "I'm coming, Eric!"

After a few seconds in the air, the jet pack started blinking. Nononono. "Eric! Where are you?!"

"OVER HERE!"

He sounded close. Come on, just a few more seconds. Blink. Blink. Blink. Gone. The jet pack disappeared for good, and I tumbled to the ground. "Eric!" I yelled. "I'm com—"

Right then, something ran into my back, pushing me to the ground and knocking the wind out of me. I turned over with an "oof" to see glowing red robot eyes staring back at me. Then another pair of eyes joined it. And a third. A scary drone thing with a claw for one hand and a drill for another started lowering toward my face.

Then the lights went out.

CHAPTER 3
Suits

Pitch-black. Hovering red eyes. Screeching, roaring, and clanking coming from thousands of evil aliens, monsters, and robots. If you know of a scarier situation, I'd love to hear it.

An emergency strobe light flashed, illuminating the still image of tall, skinny robots grabbing my arms and legs and a drone buzzing closer to my face. I kicked my legs. The light flashed again. The drone now had a buzz saw coming out of its belly. I screamed. The light flashed again. This time, the drone and its buzz saw were inches from my nose. I squeezed my eyes closed and heard a *BZZZZZZZZT!*

"NOT MY NOSE!"

BZZZT.

It wasn't my nose. Instead, my left arm dropped free from the grip of one of the robots. I dared to open my eyes, and the strobe light blinked again. Now, instead of the drone coming after me, it seemed to be going after the robot holding my right foot. Pretty soon my right foot fell to the ground. What was going on? The strobe light blinked again, showing the drone buzzing after the third robot. I heard a few scared-sounding beeps and boops; then the other two robots let go. The strobe light flashed again, and I saw all four robots running away. I sat on the ground for a few seconds to catch my breath and noticed that for the first time since this whole thing had started, the screaming computer noise was gone.

"ATTENTION!" Mr. Gregory shouted into the darkness. "THE POWER IS OFF, SO YOU CAN NOW LEAVE THROUGH THE EXIT. TAKE COVER, TAKE YOUR TIME, AND WORK TOGETHER."

I saw the exit sign way off in the distance. The strobe light flashed, lighting up a clear path through the room. I took a deep breath and started walking forward. Then the strobe light flashed again, revealing a tall, lanky robot that had just stepped out from behind one of the computer towers. I paused and waited. Another flash. The first robot was joined by another robot, and they were holding something. Another flash—the something seemed to be wiggling.

"Eric?" I yelled. "ERIC!" No answer.

One more flash. The robots were gone. I ran to where they'd been and waited for the strobe to flash again. But when it flashed—nothing. I looked down another aisle of computers. Flash. Nothing.

"ERIC!" I yelled again. No answer.

Maybe I was seeing things. Maybe Eric had made it out of the room already. I stumbled toward the glowing red exit sign, keeping watch for any robots or cockroaches or—

"SCREEEEEEECH!"

The strobe light lit up a praying mantis that had jumped right in my path. It stood on its back legs and screeched at me. Then the lights went off, and I heard a loud *BOOF!* The next strobe flash revealed my savior—a giant walking robot with a girl inside.

"Hurry!" Sam said. "I'll cover you."

I ran the rest of the way to the exit and joined dozens of other kids walking out of the room. We made it safely thanks to Sam and several others who'd hopped into robot suits to hold off the enemy horde. When I finally got out of the room, I found Mark. "Oh good, you're OK!" I said. "Have you seen Eric?"

"Not yet." He squinted in my direction. "Where is this place again?"

"Bionosoft," I said. "It's the company that trapped all of you in video games."

"They trapped us? You mean they did it on purpose?"

"Yeah," I said. "The whole thing is pretty complicated. Bionosoft really didn't want anybody to know about it, which is why we had to sneak past all these security guards . . . "

My voice trailed off when I looked down the hall. The Bionosoft security guards that I remembered from earlier had been replaced by serious men in suits. These guys looked like they'd come straight from tryouts for the Secret Service. They even wore those earpieces with the spiral wires and everything. All of the suits were busy guiding kids into a long line.

"Excuse me." I tapped one of the men on the back. "Have you seen a kid named Eric Conrad? He's about yay tall, very excitable. He's wearing a red shirt and . . . "

"I'm sorry, but you need to get in line with everyone else."

I sighed and looked back down the line. There were a LOT of kids. At that moment, Sam and Mr. Gregory emerged from the room. One of the suits talked to Mr. Gregory for a second, nodded, and swiped a key card to close the door.

"Mr. Gregory!" I yelled.

He bounded over to me with a smile on his face. "Great news!" he said. "Everybody made it out! It's a miracle!"

A wave of relief swept over me. "That's great! I was so worried about Eric!"

Mr. Gregory stopped and scrunched up his face. "You know, I actually don't remember seeing him."

"But you just said . . . "

"Everyone who was inside a computer made it out. But I could never track you or Eric because you were never in one of the computers."

I got panicky again. "So Eric could still be locked in there?"

Mr. Gregory put his hand on my shoulder. "It's OK, Jesse," he said. "There are a lot of kids here. I'm sure Eric is somewhere in the crowd. Why don't we find him right . . . "

"Excuse me." One of the suits appeared behind Mr. Gregory. "Are you Dr. Alistair Gregory?"

"I am."

"You're needed this way."

"Yes, just as soon as . . . "

"Now, please. It's a matter of national security."

"Can you just have someone help this young man find his friend?"

"Of course." With that, two suits escorted Mr. Gregory to the elevator. They did not send anyone to help me.

So then it was up to me to find Eric. Fine. I got out of line. "Eric!" I yelled. "ERIC!"

Mark joined me. "ERIC!"

We jogged in and out of the line, shouting Eric's name. We got through the whole hallway without seeing anyone who looked even remotely like Eric. Before I could check the elevator, one of the suits held out his hand. "You need to get back in line," he said.

"My friend is missing!" I said. "He's still in there! We've got to get him!"

"Everyone is accounted for. Get back in line," the man said.

"You don't understand," I replied. "He's not in the system!"

"*YOU* don't understand," Mr. Suit said. "If you don't obey, you'll be arrested for treason against the United States of America."

Treason against the United States?! What was this?

"But . . . "

The man held a walkie-talkie up to his mouth and cocked his eyebrow, daring me to make a move. Mark grabbed my arm. "Come on," he said. "Maybe we missed him."

"We didn't miss him," I whispered as we walked to the back of the line. "He's in there. I saw him."

"You saw him?!"

I nodded. "I mean, I'm pretty sure it was him." I closed my eyes for a second while I walked to replay the scene in my mind and immediately clunked foreheads with another kid. "I'm so sorry!" I said.

I looked up to see Sam rubbing her head. "I'm fine," she said. "Everything OK with you?"

"Our friend is still in there," I said.

Sam's eyes got big. "But they said everyone got out! If I would have known . . . "

"I've got to get back in there!" I said.

"But how?" Mark asked. "There's only one guy with a key card, and he's for sure not letting anyone back in there."

Sam smiled and lowered her voice. "I think I have a way," she said. Then she pulled a Super Grenade from her pocket.

CHAPTER 4
Level 1

Mark and I lost our minds when we saw the grenade.

"Relax," Sam said. She then whispered her plan. I had to admit—it was pretty good.

"But if you help me get in there, they could arrest you for treason," I said.

"What can they do to me? I'm not American."

"Well, they'll probably deport you back to England and throw you in jail and . . . "

She gave me a disgusted look. "I'm not from Britain, you ning-nong. I'm Australian."

"Oh, right," I said, my face turning red. "Of course, I just . . . "

She shook her head and walked away.

"Wait," I turned to Mark. "She's not doing it, is she?"

Sam opened one of the doors down the hall, looked inside, then moved onto the next one.

"I think she's doing it," Mark said.

I panicked a little. "I'm not ready yet!"

Sam opened another door and looked around.

"If she's in, I'm in," Mark said.

"You can't!" I whisper-yelled. "You've been missing for months! You've got to go home!"

After checking the room, Sam nodded, removed the ball from her pocket, pressed a button, and tossed it inside. She calmly walked back toward us, smiling and counting down with her fingers. Three fingers. Two fingers. One finger. She pointed at the room.

BOOM!

The door blew off its hinges, and the building shook. All the suits drew their guns and ran toward the room. As the one with the key card ran past us, Sam casually reached over and grabbed it from his belt. “Easy peasy,” she said.

While we walked to the computer room, I tried to talk Sam and Mark out of joining me. “This isn’t safe!” I hissed to Sam.

“I know!” she wiggled her eyebrows. “Isn’t it thrilling?”

I turned to Mark. “You can’t come. I—I forbid it.”

“You forbid it?” Mark asked with a smile.

“Yes. Forbid.”

Both Mark and Sam laughed as Sam swiped the key card. I tried to hold them back, but they both pushed into the room, and the door shut behind us. Inside the room, all the laughing stopped. In the dark, as we were completely surrounded by screeching, howling, and roaring, the danger suddenly felt real. The first time the strobe light flashed, I caught my breath. Without anyone to hold them back, the video game characters had torn the place apart. Sam’s robot lay on the ground in front of us in pieces. Behind that, broken computer towers littered the floor. Many of them had been dragged into a pile, forming an impressive mountain. Most of the creatures left in the room were fighting each other on the mountain, trying to win some bizarre game of King of the Hill. None of them seemed interested in us.

Sam picked up a blaster from the ground, and we slowly edged away from the door, hugging the wall behind us. After a few steps, the strobe light flashed again, and we all screamed. A buzzing thing had dropped right in front of our faces. Sam started blasting wildly.

"Stop!" I yelled. Sam blasted some more. "STOP! I know that thing!" It was the drone from earlier.

"I do, too," she said. "It's from the game I was playing!" She blasted some more.

"I don't think it's bad. It helped me earlier," I said.

"Yeah, fine," she said while searching for the drone. "That's what it's supposed to do."

"Then why are you shooting at it?!"

"Because it's the most annoying thing in the world, that's why!" She saw something move.

BLAST-BLAST.

"It follows you around everywhere beeping and whistling its stupid songs and getting in your way."

BLAST-BLAST-BLAST.

"I've spent the last week trying to blow it up in my game, and if I have to deal with it in real life, too, I think I might lose it!"

BLAST-BLAST—

"HEY!" I said as I pushed her blaster down. "We're going to need help if we want to find Eric, right? Why don't we see if it can help us?"

Silence. The strobe light flashed again, showing Sam glaring angrily like maybe she wanted to turn her blaster on me.

"That's it," I said. Then I called out to the drone. "Hey, buddy, we're not going to hurt you. Can you come out?" Nothing happened. "Buddy? Come on. It's OK, little guy." Silence.

Finally, Sam mumbled, "Its name is R.O.G.E.R."

"Roger?"

"Remote Onboarding Guide to Everything Robot," she grumbled.

"Roger? Can you help us?"

A light clicked on behind Sam and slowly peeked up over her shoulder. The drone was looking at me with its camera eye.

"That's it, buddy. We're not going to hurt you."

The drone made a cautious whistle, then peeked out a little more. When it got high enough to see the blaster in Sam's hands, however, it made a noise that sounded just like a scream and ducked back behind her.

"It's OK," I said as I slowly took the blaster from Sam and laid it on the ground. "See? Friends."

Roger peeked over again.

Bleepity-bleep?

"Yeah," I said. "It's OK."

The drone flew out of hiding and perched proudly on Mark's shoulder. Mark laughed. Sam rolled her eyes.

"That's it!" I said. "We're looking for our friend Eric. Have you seen him? He's about this tall, he's wearing a red shirt, and he kind of waddles when he runs."

The drone stared at me motionless.

"Does it understand English?" I asked Sam.

She shrugged. "It definitely doesn't understand, 'Go away.'"

I looked around for something to help me communicate with the drone, then I gasped when I saw Eric's scepter lying on the ground. "This," I said, picking it up. "Have you seen the kid who belongs to this?"

Roger stared at the scepter for a few seconds, then did a long, approving whistle.

Beep-bop!

It started flying across the room, lighting a path with its flashlight, and whistling a happy tune. I turned and gave a thumbs-up. Sam shook her head. "This is such a bad idea," she said.

Roger led us along the edge of the room, being careful to stay away from the melee in the middle. We walked and walked until the exit sign turned into a speck and the noise from King of the Hill grew faint. The strobe lights kept flashing, illuminating row upon row of black computer towers, making it feel like we were walking among tombstones. “Again, this feels like such a bad idea,” Sam said.

“Yeah,” Mark said. “How will we get back? I don’t want to . . . ”

Mark’s voice trailed off. Roger had stopped. We all gathered around as Roger pointed his flashlight at the thing we’d come for.

“What is it?” I asked.

“Looks like a hole,” Mark said.

“Yeah. A big hole. But what is it?”

Without pausing, Sam climbed into the hole. She turned around. “Level 1,” she said. “You coming?”

CHAPTER 5
Super Bot World

"What do you mean Level 1?" I shouted to Sam.

"Come down here, and I'll show you."

Mark was already crawling over the lip of the hole, so I joined him. The hole opened up into a gently sloping tunnel that we could easily walk down. Roger lit our way as we walked farther into the tunnel.

"Stay close," Sam said.

Just then, something started rumbling behind us. Mark and I caught up to Sam as the rumbling got louder. Suddenly—

CRASH!

The tunnel caved in behind us.

"What was that?!" I yelped.

"Stand over there," Sam said. Mark and I quickly obeyed.

Three short robots with snapping claws emerged from the dust of the cave-in and started lunging toward us. Sam ran right at them.

"Sam! No!" I called after her.

Just before one of the robots could claw her, she jumped onto its head.

POP!

It disappeared. She used the momentum from that jump to hop onto the next robot—*POP!*—and the next. *POP!* Roger did a victory whistle as Sam walked back to us.

"Save it," Sam muttered to Roger as she continued down the tunnel.

Mark and I stared at her speechless. "Do you want to let us know what's going on yet?" I finally asked.

"*Super Bot World 3*," she said.

I looked at Mark. He shrugged.

"Um, what's *Super Bot World 3*?" I asked.

"The bots, the tunnel, the cave-in. This buzzard." Sam pointed at Roger. "Everything's from *Super Bot World 3*. You've played *Super Bot World 3*, haven't you?"

"I've played no *Super Bod Worlds*," Mark said.

"*Super* Bod *World*?" Sam squinted at him.

"Oh, wait, are you saying 'bot'? Like 'robot'?" I asked.

Sam looked at each of us to see if we were joking. "Yeah," she finally said. "*Super Bot*," she made sure to emphasize the *t*, *"World 3*. It's only the biggest game in the world."

"Never heard of it," Mark said.

"Well, at least it's the biggest game in Australia. I've been trapped inside of it for the last week."

Sam stopped at a metal cube lying on the ground and pressed a glowing red button on top of the cube. It transformed inside out around her hand, giving her a giant metal fist.

"So you're saying as soon as these robots got out of their game, they started building it again in the real world?" I asked.

"Looks like it. This is an exact replica of the first level."

"But why?"

Sam held up her finger for us to wait, and the ground started rumbling. After a second, a crazed robot with gears for eyes popped out of the dirt in front of us. Sam bopped the robot on the head like a whack-a-mole. "They're bots." She continued walking as if nothing had happened. "Bots do what they're programmed to do. If they're supposed to build complicated levels and kidnap the princess, they'll do it no matter where they are."

"Time out," I said. "What do you mean . . . "

Sam reached around me and punched a robot that had just popped out of the wall on my left.

" . . . What do you mean 'kidnap the princess'?"

"I don't know; that's the dumb story in this game. The evil robot overlords capture the robot princess and take her away because of her heart of gold or some junk like that. It's like *Mario*." She looked sideways at us. "You do have *Mario* here, right?"

I glanced at the scepter in my hand. Upon closer inspection, it did look like something that a robot princess might have. "So if they saw Eric with the scepter . . . "

"Yeah, they probably thought he was the princess," Sam said.

I dropped the scepter and started to panic. “So what are they going to do to him? Where are they taking him? Do they want to rip out his heart of gold?!”

“Relax,” Sam said. “They’re building this level as they go, remember? I’m sure we’ll catch up before they get too far.”

“We’re not going to catch anybody walking like this!” I said as I started to run. “Let’s go!”

I got about 20 yards before I realized nobody was following me. I turned to see Roger shining his light on part of the tunnel wall for Sam.

“What are you doing?!” I yelled back.

Sam clunked Roger on the head, and he moved the light closer to her. She tapped the dirt a couple of times, then wound up with her metal fist and punched right through the wall.

“Coming?” she called out to me.

I jogged back to her and Mark. “What’s this?”

She stepped through the hole into the darkness. All of a sudden, a series of lights clicked on in front of us, revealing a mine cart track set over a bottomless pit.

“It’s a shortcut,” Sam said.

CHAPTER 6
Mine Cart Madness

Mark and Sam started climbing into the mine cart. "Wait!" I said. "That doesn't look big enough for three people."

Sam stuck her giant metal hand out of the cart as she sat down, giving Mark space to squeeze in behind her. "Look, plenty of room," she said. Mark scrunched himself as small as he could, providing enough room for maybe a baby to fit behind him.

"I'm just saying, if anybody falls out or if that thing tips over, we're not magically reappearing at the beginning of the level," I said. "We're dead. Dead-dead. Like real-life dead. Wouldn't it be a lot safer to take the long way through the level?"

"My leg's falling asleep," Sam said. "Are you getting in or what?"

"But . . . "

"The longer you putz around, the more time these bots have to build their killing machines. Just get in the blasted cart!"

I sighed and squeezed behind Mark. There wasn't enough room to sit down inside the cart, so I had to settle for wedging my feet underneath Mark and sitting on the back lip of the cart. Roger landed on top of my head.

"This is going to be a real ripper!" Sam released the brake. "It's just like a roller coaster!"

She was wrong. It was not just like a roller coaster because roller coasters don't make you hold on to keep yourself from falling into a bottomless pit every time you go over a hill.

"Slow down!" I yelled the first time I almost popped out of the cart.

"No can do," Sam said.

"WHY NOT?!"

"That's why not." Sam pointed ahead to a missing section of track.

That's another nice feature of roller coasters—they generally have all their tracks.

"AHHHHHH!" I screamed as we approached the giant pit. At the last second, Sam pounded a button at the front of the cart, causing a small rocket to pop out of the mine cart and boost us over the hole in the tracks. We landed just on the edge of the next set of tracks.

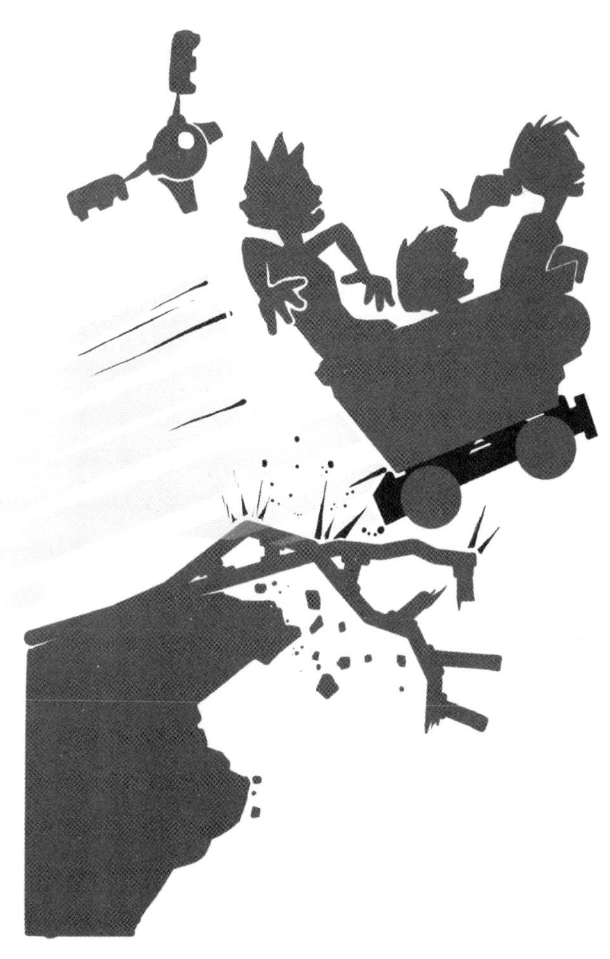

"Woo-hoo!" Mark yelled. "That was awesome!"

Sam, for once, didn't join in the excitement. Instead, she turned around to give us the first worried look I'd seen from her all day. "The booster usually gets you a lot farther than that," she said. "There might be too much weight in the cart."

"Is that going to be a problem?" I asked.

Instead of answering, Sam turned around just in time to hit the boosters for the next set of missing tracks. This time when we blasted off, there were no other tracks in sight—only a helicopter robot hovering in our path. "Everyone lean back!" Sam instructed. We all leaned, pulling the front of our mine cart up just enough to clip the enemy. That gave us the momentum we needed to barely make it to the next set of tracks.

These tracks were angled like the first hill of a roller coaster. We picked up more and more speed until the tracks bottomed out and turned into a ski jump ramp. Our cart launched high into the air, and Sam started hitting the boost button over and over. Even with the big jump and repeated rocket boosts, it became clear that we weren't going to make it to the next set of tracks.

"What do we do?!" Mark yelled.

Beepity booooooop!

Roger made a "Superman saves the day" sound and flew off of my head as if lightening the load by three pounds was going to make a difference. But Roger seemed to be thinking of more than just his own weight. He hovered inches over my head and blooped and squawked and made car alarm sounds until I grabbed him. As soon as I had a grip, his four tiny propellers began working overtime. He started pulling me up just a little. I clenched my knees around Mark, and Mark held tight to the mine cart.

CLANK!

It was the closest call yet, but we somehow landed back on the tracks. We continued jumping and boosting and bouncing off of enemies, but I could feel a growing sense of dread from the front of the cart. "What's wrong, Sam?"

When she turned around, her face was white. "We're not going to make it."

"What do you mean?" I asked. "Roger can help. Even if it's a really big jump, we should be fine . . . "

"NO!" she interrupted. "The last part is a jump through a closing door. We need speed, not height! With all this weight in the cart, we're just too slow."

Mark and I remained silent as we sped down the track.

"I was so stupid," Sam said. "I don't know why I made you both do this."

We jumped another pit, then found ourselves speeding down a hill. At the end of the hill was a ramp, and past that ramp was a slowly lowering metal slab.

"Could two people make it?" Mark asked.

"What do you mean?" Sam said.

"If only two people were in the cart, would it be light enough to make the jump?"

We were rolling so fast now that I could barely keep my eyes open against the wind. "It doesn't matter," Sam said. "There's no way . . . "

Mark stopped listening. He had made up his mind. He spun around, put his hands on my shoulders, and jumped out of the cart.

CHAPTER 7
Diggin' Season

"MARK! NO!"

He landed on the tracks and tumbled a few times. I reached for him, but it was too late—we'd run out of track. Sam and I launched into the air.

Roger flew behind the cart and pushed it as hard as he could. By now, the giant door had nearly closed. Even with Mark's sacrifice, it didn't look like we'd make it. I watched Mark tumble down the track until he finally rolled to a stop just before the pit.

"GET DOWN!"

I turned back around to see Sam in my face. She yanked me into the mine cart right before we squeaked underneath the door. As soon as the cart crashed and we spilled out, both of us ran back to the door and tried to lift it. It wouldn't budge. We pounded and pounded, but the metal was so thick that it barely made a thud. Roger finally tried his buzz saw, but even that got nothing but sparks.

As the minutes ticked by, I grew more frustrated. I'd almost gotten killed 20 different times trying to rescue Mark, and just as soon as we'd broken him out of his video game prison, Sam had buried him in an underground tomb because she wanted to go on a stupid roller-coaster ride. I started walking away.

"Wait, we've got to help Matt!" Sam said.

I spun around. "Mark! His name's Mark! You got him killed, and you don't even know his name." I turned and stalked away.

She finally caught up to me. "I'm sorry about Mark," she said quietly.

"Yeah. Me, too," I muttered. "I just hope we survive long enough to get him some help."

She hung her head, and we walked silently for a while. Sam punched robots here and there with her metal fist, but there was no longer any joy in it. We eventually came across another metal box with a glowing red button. "We're almost to the boss," Sam said. "You're going to need that."

I pressed the button, and a helmet formed over my head. "What's this for?"

"Protection."

We walked a little farther, and our narrow tunnel opened up into an enormous cavern with stalactites on the ceiling. It was pretty impressive. "So you're telling me the robots built all this, too?" I asked.

Sam shrugged. "You should see some of these bots."

Suddenly, a giant metal cube fell from the darkness above. The cube buzzed and whirred and opened up like a Transformer until it was a 15-foot-tall robot with a long tube contraption attached to its right arm. It was terrifying.

"What does that do?!" I screamed.

Before Sam could answer, the robot jammed the tube into the ground and fired. A shockwave rippled through the cavern, knocking us off balance and causing a cave-in back where we'd entered. The robot roared and started slowly walking toward us. Words flickered on my helmet visor.

BUILD: DGN-SZN

POWER: 88

SPEED: 39

INTELLIGENCE: 11

VULNERABILITY: HEAD

"OK, uh, the build looks like dig, uh, diggun sizzin? Diggin . . . "

"I don't care about any of that," Sam said, her eyes on the ceiling.

I looked up to see Roger buzzing in and out of the stalactites. He finally stopped at one he liked and pointed his light at it.

"Come on!" Sam said. We ran underneath the stalactite and waited. The robot plodded toward us. Even when it started getting close, Sam refused to move.

"Sam?" I said. The robot was close enough that I could feel a gust of wind every time it took a step.

"Not yet."

The robot got closer. I could now see up its robot nose.

"SAM?!"

"Wait for it."

When the robot was just one step away, it jumped.

"NOW!" Sam sprinted away from the robot. She didn't have to tell me twice. I was already halfway across the cavern when the robot landed on the spot where we'd been standing. When it hit the ground, it put its tube thing into the dirt and fired again. This time, there was an even bigger shockwave, and I felt the *tink-tink-tink* of tiny rocks from the ceiling hitting my helmet. Sam held her metal fist above her head to protect herself.

CRASH!

The stalactite that we'd been standing under earlier broke loose and fell onto the robot's head. He stumbled backward and roared again. Roger pointed his flashlight at another stalactite across the room. "We've got to move faster now," Sam said.

I followed her underneath the stalactite and waited for the robot to come at us again. When he jumped this time, I got a bad start and twisted my ankle.

"Ah!" I yelled as I hobbled to Sam.

"You OK?" she asked.

Before I could answer, the robot sent another shockwave, knocking us to the ground. Pebbles from the ceiling pelted me again, and—

CRASH!

We scored another direct hit.

When I stood back up, my ankle started throbbing. "This is bad," I said as I hopped backward and stumbled around. Sam put her nonmetal hand around me and guided me to the third stalactite.

The robot got up, roared, and practically ran at us.

"Sam?" I said. "I don't think I'm going to be able to do this again."

"Trust me," she said as she put her metal fist on my back.

Based on recent experience, that was not an easy instruction to follow. I waited as long as I could, then started hobbling away.

"Jesse! Wait!"

Sam stood under the stalactite a half second longer, then lunged and punched me across the room with her supercharged fist. By saving me, Sam didn't have any time left to get to safety herself. She rolled away from the robot's foot at the last second but couldn't use her metal hand to protect herself from falling debris. I helplessly watched as she scrunched into a ball while rocks from the ceiling hit her. Finally, the stalactite fell onto the robot, causing him to stumble a few times before finally falling over for good.

I ran to Sam, who had bruises and scrapes all over her body. "Are you OK?!"

She groaned and nodded. Then she pointed to the fallen robot's shockwave blaster. "I think I know how we can rescue Mark."

CHAPTER 8
Lefty Loosey

We got to work unscrewing the robot's blaster from its arm. Actually, Sam did the unscrewing with her super-strong metal hand. Roger provided light, and I mostly watched and made dumb suggestions.

"Lefty loosey, righty tighty," I said when she was struggling with one especially tough screw.

"I knoooow," she replied, adding a bunch of *r*'s at the end of "know" in a very Australian way.

"So how is this going to help us rescue Mark again?" I asked.

"We use it to break the door."

"Yeah, but then what?"

"We'll figure it out, OK?"

WHACK!

"OW!" Sam shook out her nonmetal hand, which she'd just jammed with a screw. "ROGER, STOP WANDERING OFF WITH THE TORCH!"

Roger, who had been slowly losing interest in the project, quickly turned his flashlight back to Sam.

"I can't wait to take you to the scrapyard," Sam muttered.

I paused for a second. "Hey, do you hear that?"

"Hear what?"

"That rumbling sound."

Sam shrugged. "The next level is a sewer. It's probably water."

"It doesn't sound like water, though," I said. "It's like, I don't know, it's extra rumbly."

"Go have a lookie if you like," Sam said without looking up. "The tunnel to the next level is over there."

I followed her finger, and sure enough, a hole just big enough to crawl through had opened up on the other side of the cavern. I jogged over and peeked in. When I did, the sound got louder, and I got a distinct whiff of diesel fuel. I crawled inside, waited for my eyes to adjust to the darkness, and then navigated around a corner. When I turned the corner, I glimpsed the cause of the rumbling and immediately stumbled backward.

It was them.

The tall, skinny robots I'd seen at Bionosoft were marching down the tunnel, carrying something squirmy and Eric-shaped. In front of them was an army of tanks, drilling machines, and scary robot soldiers. I crawled back to the cavern as fast as I could.

"Sam!" I yelled.

Roger looked up.

"What did I say about the torch?!" Sam snapped. Roger quickly went back to lighting the robot for Sam.

"I found Eric!"

Roger shrieked with delight and started flying toward me.

"OK," Sam said without looking. "Almost got this."

"It doesn't matter! Did you hear what I said? We need to get Eric!"

"Not now," she said, still tinkering away.

Roger stopped in midair. He looked confused.

"WHAT DO YOU MEAN NOT NOW?!"

Sam finally sat up and looked me in the eye. Oil and dirt had joined the scratches and bruises on her face. "These things disappear if you leave them for too long," she calmly explained as she patted the robot. "If I don't get the blaster off now, we might not ever be able to reach Mark."

I stared at her in disbelief. "This is real life! Not a video game! NOTHING'S GOING TO DISAPPEAR!"

"I can't take that chance," Sam said.

"What are you talking about?! Eric is right here!"

"I got Mark into this mess, so it's on me to get him back out. Trust me; your mate will be fine for a few more minutes."

I couldn't believe what I was hearing. "Would you stop feeling guilty for one second and help me?!"

Sam went back to working on the robot. Roger looked at Sam, then at me, then back at Sam.

"Ouch!" Sam shouted as she hit her finger again. "Roger, you are SECONDS away from scrap!" Roger immediately returned to light her work.

Fine, I didn't need them anyway. I turned back in a huff and crawled toward the rumbling. When I rounded the corner this time, I noticed that the robot army was gone. In its place was a perfectly circular hole at the end of the tunnel. I walked to the opening and took a deep breath for courage. Then I gagged. The robots had indeed drilled through to the very real, very smelly city sewer system. I put my shirt over my nose and peeked out.

The hole overlooked a fast-flowing river of muck and filth. Down below, hundreds of robots were busy rebuilding the level they remembered. Orange construction vehicles carved out nooks and crannies. Tall, walking box things rumbled their way down the river, dropping off enemies every few feet. Elsewhere, black drones flew around, stringing electrical wiring and adding lights.

It was all kinds of beautiful. I could have watched the robots build their new level all day if it weren't for the squirming thing one of the tall, skinny robots was carrying upside down. In the light, I could clearly see it was Eric, still kicking and yelling with every step the robot took.

I wanted to run down to rescue him right there or at least yell to let him know it was OK, but I couldn't risk drawing attention to myself with all these robots around, especially while I was unarmed. I looked for something I could use to help Eric.

Bloop!

My helmet made a noise, and a floating red circle appeared over a prize cube on the walkway next to the sewage river. "AQUA COMBAT BOOTS" appeared in red letters on my visor, and an arrow pointed to the cube. OK, that was a start. I edged a little farther onto the lookout to check out the river underneath me. If I could just find another prize cube or maybe a . . .

BAM!

Something whacked me hard in the head, causing stars to flash in front of my eyes. While I tried to figure out what had happened, I got pinched on the leg. "Mmrmph!" I let out a muffled scream to keep from alerting the robots underneath. Another pinch. "MMMRRRMMMMPH!"

I looked down to see a mechanical spider the size of my head tormenting me. I tried to throw it off the ledge, but when I reached for it—

BAM!

Another spider jumped from the ceiling and landed on my visor. I stumbled around in full panic mode, unable to see a thing.

BAM!

Another spider hit me in the chest. When I tried to rip it off, I took a step backward, rolled my bad ankle on the first spider, and completely lost my balance. I clawed wildly for something—anything—to keep me upright, but it was no good. I fell off the ledge.

CHAPTER 9
The Pit of Despair

I fell and fell and fell some more, and just when I thought that surely this was the end of the falling—nope—the falling continued. I curled up and prepared to do a cannonball into the smelly water, but the water never came. Instead, I crashed through some boards on the walkway next to the river. Then I fell even more. Finally, I landed with a gigantic *SQUISH*.

After a few seconds, I realized that I wasn't dead and opened my eyes. I had fallen on top of one of the robot spiders (which was now quite dead) inside a squishy mud pit. When I looked up, I could just barely make out a thin stream of light 30 feet above me. I tried to move. Although my entire body was sore and covered with mud, all of my limbs seemed to work OK. I looked around for some sort of ladder or rope. Nothing. The pit was pretty narrow, so I tried to Spider-Man crawl my way up. I just slipped back down. I wanted to yell for help, but the only thing that would accomplish would be attracting every robot in the sewer to my location.

I crumpled at the bottom of the pit and—don't tell anyone—started to cry. Hard. Like that cry where you're not able to catch your breath, so in addition to being really sad, you're also a little panicky because you can't quite breathe. In the span of two hours, I had lost two friends and buried myself deep inside a smelly sewer. I was tired and cold and alone. On top of all that, I just remembered that this whole day had begun with me unable to eat breakfast. I was starving.

Suddenly, a noise above interrupted my pity party. Footsteps! Then, one of the boards moved!

"Sam!" I yelled. "SAM!"

But it wasn't Sam. Instead, a metallic face looked down at me. I put my hand over my mouth, and we stared at each other for a few seconds. Then the robot pushed the board back over the hole, making his level perfect again and sealing off my last chance for rescue.

I stared in disbelief for a while longer, then curled into a ball and positioned the broken spider robot under my head for a pillow. Might as well get comfortable. I cried myself to sleep.

CHAPTER 10
Blast Number Three

Poke.

I kept my eyes closed.

Poke poke.

Don't you hate it when your mom wakes you up for school by poking you? Yelling is fine because you can always "Mmmmf coming" your way to a few extra minutes, but moms don't stop poking until your butt has left the bed.

"Mmmmf, coming," I tried.

Poke poke poke.

"OK, OK." I rolled over to get out of my nice, warm bed. Except I didn't get out of bed. Instead, I just squished into more mud. All of a sudden, I remembered where I was. "Mmmmmmmmf!"

Poke-poke, poke-poke.

If I wasn't in bed, then what was poking me? Just then, a light flashed in my face. I squinted and saw a small drone hovering next to me, preparing to poke again. "Roger?"

Beep-beep beepity booooooooooop!

Roger made a happy loop in the air. Sam's face appeared in the hole. "Jesse? Is that you down there?"

"Sam?!"

Beepity booooooooooop!

"No way!" Sam said. "This is bonkers! Positively BONKERS! Wowwy! OK, hold on while we find a rope or something."

Roger zipped back up to the top and joined Sam. Ten minutes later, they returned. "Well," Sam said. "We can get you out, but you're not going to like it." She explained that they'd found some rope, but it wasn't long enough to reach me. What they'd have to do instead was divert the sewer water into my hole and float me to the top.

"So your plan is to pour thousands of gallons of sewage onto my head?"

"Roger found something for you to hang onto," Sam said.

Roger did a very proud "beep-beep" and pushed a dirty beach ball down into the hole.

"Thanks," I said sarcastically. Roger made a thumbs-up with his claw.

Sam and Roger disappeared. A few seconds later, I heard a *chink-chink-chink-CHUNK*. On the *CHUNK*, smelly sewer water started gushing into my hole. I covered my head to protect myself from the ickiness but eventually gave up and held onto the beach ball as I floated to the top like a drowned rat. When I finally flopped out of the hole, Roger cheered.

Beepity beeeeeeeeeeep!

He circled me while whistling the same happy tune over and over.

"Thank you," I said to Sam. "That was—I just can't believe you found me."

"No worries," Sam said as she helped me up. "I found this for you to dry off with if you want." She held out a disgusting rag.

"I'll air-dry, thanks."

Sam led me back to the cavern while explaining what had happened. After I'd left, she'd gotten the shockwave blaster off the robot's arm, but it turned out to be way too heavy to carry herself. Sam then tried finding me but figured out pretty quickly that I'd gone missing. She panicked and scoured every inch of the sewer before Roger finally noticed the plank that had been moved.

"How long was I down there?" I asked.

"A few hours, I think."

"A few hours?! They could be anywhere by now!"

"I know," Sam said. "That's why we've just got to focus on helping Mark now."

We trekked back to the big shockwave blaster. "OK, you pick up this side, and I'll take that side," Sam said. "Together, I think we can drag it back to the door." We got into position. "One, two, three, heave-ho!"

We moved the blaster a foot. After a half hour of heaving and hoeing the blaster foot by foot through the tunnel, we finally reached the door. Sam positioned the mouth of the blaster on the door, moved to the trigger on the back, and took a quick breather before shouting "Here goes!" and pulling the trigger.

The blaster hummed, then whirred, then—

POW!

It blew the door into oblivion. Sam ran through. "Mark! Mark, are you there?!"

Roger flew ahead with his flashlight, illuminating a balled-up lump on the tracks.

"MARK!"

The lump lifted its head. Mark squinted at us. "Guys? H-how . . . "

"Don't worry, buddy," I shouted across the chasm. "We're coming! Sam has a plan!"

"Well, I don't know about 'plan,'" Sam whispered to me.

"You don't have a plan?"

"I figured something would present itself when we got here."

"OK," I shouted back to Mark. "No plan yet, but we're working on it!"

"What are we going to do?" I asked Sam. "We can't jump. We can't fly. Roger's not big enough to carry him over."

Sam wasn't paying attention. She was staring at the ceiling. "What if we crumble it?" she said.

"Crumble what?"

"The ceiling. What if we crumble it? We could use the blaster to make the ceiling fall like we did back there."

I stared at her with my mouth hanging open.

"See that crack in the ceiling?" she continued. "If it crumbles along that crack, the cave-in will fall into the pit and maybe make enough of a bridge for Mark to walk to us."

I stared for a few more seconds to make sure she was serious before offering my opinion. "That sounds like a great plan if you'd like to crush us all," I finally said.

"Oh yeah, well, what's your great idea?"

I had no great ideas. So after arguing about it for a while longer, we finally decided to "give it a go" as Sam put it. We used rocks as a wedge to get the blaster pointed at the ground; then Roger flew my helmet over to Mark for protection.

"Blast number one!" Sam shouted from on top of the blaster.

POW!

The ground shook, and a few rocks fell from the ceiling, but that was it.

"Blast number two!"

POW!

A few more rocks fell.

"Turn up the dial," I suggested.

Sam nodded and tinkered with the blaster a bit. "Blast number three!"

POW!

The shockwave sent me to the ground and Sam off the blaster. Bigger rocks fell from the ceiling, but still nothing big. Then the cave started rumbling.

"Do you feel that?" Sam asked.

The rumbling got louder. The ceiling cracked.

"TAKE COVER!"

CRAAAAAAAACK! BOOM!

I scrambled just as the ceiling started tumbling down. The crashing lasted for a good 30 seconds before everything went silent. I waited a few more seconds before opening my eyes; then I immediately had to close them again with all the dust in the air. "Mark!" I yelled into the darkness. "Are you OK?"

"More than OK!" Mark shouted back. "Check it out!"

I squinted and saw that against all odds, Sam's plan had worked. Somehow, the cave-in had filled the pit with enough rubble to form a rocky path from the mine cart track to the ledge. Up above, fluorescent office light streamed in through a hole in the ceiling. We'd managed to blow a hole all the way up to Bionosoft without crushing anyone. It was a *Super Bot World* miracle.

"Let's move before anything else comes down!" Sam said.

Mark whooped as he climbed to the edge of the tracks and jumped onto a chunk of concrete.

"Hey!"

Mark stopped and looked up. We followed his eyes. One of the men in suits from earlier was standing at the top of the hole.

"Don't move."

CHAPTER 11
Glug

Another suit joined the first one. "I think that's one of them," he said. "Can you take off that helmet so we can talk to you?" he called down to Mark. "Where are the other two?"

Sam and I edged back into a shadow before they could see us. Mark did not take off his helmet. "They're looking for our friend," he said.

"Your friend's fine," the first suit assured him. "Everyone made it. We checked the records. Now—this is very important—have you told anybody what happened to you?"

"They have our friend," Mark repeated, a little agitated. "The robots have our friend, and we need to find him."

That caught the suits' attention. "What robots?"

"The robots from the game. They escaped, and they're getting away."

That was enough for Suit Number One. He spoke into his radio as he jogged away. “We have a containment issue,” he said. “Ready the explosives.”

“Explosives?!” Mark yelled. “They have our friend! Hey!”

“We understand that this is a serious situation,” Suit Number Two said. “We’re getting you to safety, but first, it’s very important that you . . . ”

Before the suit could finish the “very important” part, Mark shook his head and walked across the rubble bridge.

“Wait! Stop!” The guy pulled out his radio. “He’s on the move! Send in a team!”

“Let’s get out of here,” Mark said as he stomped past us.

Sam and Roger followed him. I tried to keep up with my bad ankle. “Hey, guys, don’t you think we should talk to them? Remember that treason thing from before?”

“Remember that explosives thing from just now?” Sam replied as she squeezed into the tunnel that led to the sewer.

We all followed behind. Just as I ducked into the tunnel, I heard boots in the cavern. “They’re coming,” I whispered. We all ran a little faster.

When we emerged from the tunnel, Sam punched two robot spiders before I even saw them. “You two go ahead,” she said, smiling at her metal fist. “I’ve got a surprise for those guys.”

“No way,” I said. “We stick together now.”

Sam gave me a weird look. “Since when?”

“Since splitting up didn’t work out for us last time.”

Sam rolled her eyes.

“Can you get us through this level?” Mark asked.

“Well, there are two ways to do it,” she said. “There’s the safe way and the fast way.”

“Fast way,” Mark said.

Sam nodded. “I agree.” She looked at me.

On the one hand, the last “fast way” is what got us into this mess in the first place. On the other hand, I imagined things might get even worse if the suits caught up with us. I took a deep breath. “Let’s do it.”

“Good on you!” Sam gave me a playful punch on the arm with her metal fist. It hurt a lot. We took an elevator platform down, and Sam picked up a few planks from the hole I’d fallen into earlier. “Board or ski?” she asked me.

“I’d prefer neither.”

“You ski; I’ll board,” she said, grabbing three planks. “Now where was that rope? Ah, here we go.” Then she took all her supplies to the power-up cube I’d seen earlier.

Mark was looking at the cube through his helmet. “Aqua combat boots?” he said. “Do you want to tell us what you’re doing?”

“Turning you into a speedboat,” Sam replied as she looped the rope around Mark’s waist a few times. She turned to me, holding out one end of the rope. “Grab this and step onto those boards.”

I gave her an uneasy look.

"You asked for the fast way!" she said. "Roger! Tape!"

Roger duct-taped my feet to the boards, then moved onto Sam's board.

Mark looked down at the questionable skis. "Are those going to hold up?" he asked. "What if . . . "

"THERE!"

We all looked up. Five suits had made it to the overlook.

Sam grabbed the other end of the rope. "Hit that button and jump in!"

She didn't need to tell Mark twice. He hit the button on the cube in front of him, and it instantly transformed into rocket-powered boots that wrapped around his feet. He took a deep breath and jumped into the river of sewage, dragging us with him.

"I don't know anything about waterskiing!" I managed to say before falling in and getting a mouthful of sewer water.

"Lean back!" Sam called out from her wakeboard.

I struggled to do anything but hold onto the rope and flop in the water. Something clamped onto one of my legs.

SMASH!

Sam leaned over and punched what looked like a robot piranha. She then pushed me upright. “I SAID LEAN BACK!” she said.

“Lean back?” Mark asked.

“NOT YOU!”

Too late. We were already flying through the air. Mark came back down on the head of another robot piranha, and I came back down mouth-first in a river of sewage. To be honest, I can’t describe much of the rest of our journey down the sewer, because I spent most of it flopping in sewer water like a floppy fish. Here are all the things I heard when my head wasn’t underwater:

GLUG, GLUG, GLUG.

“Turn left here! I said left! Are you deaf?! LEF—”

GLUG, GLUG, GLUG.

“Why don’t you just drive if you know everything?!”

GLUG, GLUG, GLUG.

"ROGER, GET OUT OF MY FACE!"

Finally, after what felt like an hour of flopping and glugging, we jumped our last ramp and tumbled to a stop in another tunnel. I stumbled around on my skis for a couple of seconds until Roger cut them off. "Can we not do the fast way anymore?" I asked before puking all over the ground.

Sam and Mark patiently waited for me to empty my stomach of sewer water before pressing forward into the next room. "Whoa," Mark said as we walked to the middle of the chamber. The walls created a perfect circle around us, and the ceiling was at least 100 feet high. It felt like we were standing inside the world's biggest Pringles can. Right in front of us was a power-up cube.

"Why don't you take this one, Jesse?" Mark asked.

I smiled and walked to the cube, excited to see what sweet ability I'd get. Body armor would be nice. Maybe one of those big fists. I pressed the button, and the cube transformed into a—boomerang?

A door slammed behind us, and I started to panic. "I don't know how to use one of these!" I said. "Sam, shouldn't you have taken this?!"

"Why, because I'm Australian?"

"No, I just . . . "

"You think all Aussies are boomerang experts? Maybe we get one when we're born and start hunting roos straightaway? Is that it?!"

"No, literally I just thought . . . "

"Can you show me how to ride a bucking bronco, partner?" Sam said in a bad American accent. "Why not; you're American?!" She finally paused to take a breath and glare at me.

"I just meant that you've played this game before," I said.

"Oh." Sam had not considered this possibility. "Well, it's quite simple, really. The boomerang is rocket-powered, so you just have to . . . "

BOOOOM!

Sam's explanation got cut short by a giant metal spider landing inches from our faces.

CHAPTER 12
Pringles and Piranhas

Don't tell anyone, but I'm secretly afraid of spiders. I don't really know what most of the poisonous ones look like, so I'm always a little nervous that every spider I see is going to kill me. It's not like spiders make me scream or jump on a chair or anything, but any bravery you might see from me during a standard spider showdown is definitely fake.

This time there was no bravery, even the fake kind. There was lots of screaming. The robot spider in front of us was the size of an elephant and furious. So very furious. Also, it had a glowing hourglass on its back, which is the one poisonous spider symbol I know.

The *THUD* it made when it dropped to the ground caused a metal slab to fall behind us. "Get on that!" Sam shouted. We all obeyed.

The spider looked us up and down with all of its creepy robot spider eyes and jumped onto the wall to our right. It tapped on the wall a few times, then wound up and pierced right through it, causing water to start gushing out. Then the spider jumped across the room and did the same thing on the other side. Water quickly covered the floor and lifted our piece of metal. The spider worked its way around the room, poking holes in the wall and causing more water to flood the room. Soon, robot piranhas began shooting out of the holes, too. One flopped onto our metal slab, and Sam smashed it with her fist. Others landed in the water and poked their heads out to watch us.

"I'll take care of anything that lands on here!" Sam shouted. "Mark, use your boots to run onto the water and jump on the piranhas!"

"What do I do?" I asked. At that moment, Roger started beeping and squawking.

Sam looked up. The spider was resting on the ceiling, its hourglass glowing brighter than ever. "Use the boomerang! Now!"

"What, you want me to boomerang the spider?"

"Yes!" A piranha jumped onto our platform. *BOOF!* Sam clocked it. "Of course!" *BOOF!* "What else would you do?" *BOOF!*

I looked back at the ceiling, but it was too late—the spider had moved on.

“UNG!” Sam said. “NO DAWDLING!”

The spider continued poking more holes in the wall, which let in more water, which caused us to rise faster. After half a minute of poking, it jumped to the ceiling again. I closed one eye, squinted with the other, and aimed the best I could. Finally, I threw the boomerang. Not even close.

“JESSE!” Sam yelled.

“I’m not good at aiming!”

More holes. More water. More piranhas. The spider jumped back to the ceiling. I aimed again, knowing that I was basically guessing. Then, just before I threw the boomerang, Sam took a quick break from smashing piranhas to throw me closer to my target with her robot hand. At the height of my arc, I let the boomerang fly. Direct hit! The spider beat on the ceiling a few times and jumped back on the wall.

"Good on you!" Sam shouted.

The piranhas had begun coming so fast that Sam didn't even have time to look at me during her congratulations. Also, we were now about two-thirds of the way up the room and picking up speed. This time when the spider jumped to the ceiling, Sam didn't need to throw me because I was close enough to hit it easily for the second time.

The spider got madder. It jumped on the wall and started banging huge holes with its head. Water and piranhas gushed into the room. "I can't keep up with all of them!" Mark yelled from the water.

"It's fine; just take off your boots!" Sam shouted.

"What?! No way!"

"Just do it!"

With all the new water pouring in, we had begun rocketing toward the ceiling. We were moments away from death by either squishing or drowning. As the spider finished its last head bashing, Mark ran to the metal slab and tore off his boots. The spider jumped to the ceiling right above our heads.

"Into the water!" Sam shouted.

Mark looked down at the piranha-infested water, then up at the fast-approaching ceiling.

"I don't . . . "

SPLASH!

Sam pushed him. She followed him into the water; then Roger followed her. I waited as long as I could for the spider's hourglass to light up, but I'd run out of time. I jumped off of the slab a half second before my head hit the spider. While I was in midair, the hourglass lit up. I threw the boomerang and splashed into the water before I could tell whether I'd hit it. Underwater, I could see that Sam, Mark, and Roger were swimming straight down, so I joined them. One-two-three strokes down and—

BOOM!

A shockwave rippled through the water. I looked up to see that the spider had exploded, ripping a hole in the ceiling. Suddenly, I got sucked upward.

CHAPTER 13
Impossible Mode

For the second time in one day (and, coincidentally, also the second time in my life), I got pushed out of a pit by sewer water. I flopped onto the ground next to a fountain of filthy sewage and looked around to see that we'd been spit out in the middle of the woods, under a moonlit sky.

"Is everyone OK?" I asked after coughing out a mouthful of water.

"Ung," Sam said.

"Ung," Mark said.

Bloooooooooorg, Roger said.

We all tried our best to wring out our clothes before giving up and resigning ourselves to sloshing all evening. Mark noticed the bulldozer tracks first.

"What are those?" he asked.

Several sets of tracks cleared a path through the forest. Sam sighed. “They go to the next level, I’m sure.” She got up. “Coming?”

“Wait,” I said. “So these tracks probably lead to a horrible place . . . ”

“It’s a factory,” Sam interrupted.

“They lead to a horrible factory filled with death bots, while the robots that have Eric will probably be long gone.”

Sam shrugged. “Probably.”

“So wouldn’t it be smarter to skip the factory and catch up to Eric a few levels ahead?”

Sam shrugged again. “Probably.”

I stopped for a second, stunned that Sam had finally agreed with me about something. “So, uh, why don’t we just do that?”

“Because I don’t know what comes next.”

“Excuse me?”

“I. Don’t. Know. What. Comes. Next.” Sam exaggerated each word in the sentence.

“I thought you were in this game for a week!” I said.

"I was," Sam replied. "And I only made it to the third level, OK?"

Suddenly, I had a lot less faith in the person who was supposed to guide us. I gave Mark an "uh-oh" glance.

Sam saw the look. "Hey, I'm good at this stuff, OK? I love video games, so I always play on 'impossible' difficulty to make them last longer. It just turns out that *Super Bot World 3* has a really impossible 'impossible' mode."

"So not only are we going to be fighting blind after this level, but we'll also face impossible robots?" Mark asked.

Sam shrugged a third time.

I suddenly felt overwhelmed and guilty. "Hey, guys," I said. "Thanks for coming, but you two need to leave now. This is my thing, and I couldn't live with myself if something happened to either of you."

"And you think we'd be fine if something happened to you?" Mark asked.

"Yeah," Sam said. "We stick together now, remember?" She said that sentence in her bad American accent, I guess doing an impression of me.

Before I could argue, we reached a clearing that revealed our town's old paper mill. The mill was a rusty old factory that had been dark and spooky ever since it was abandoned 20 years ago, but not tonight. Tonight, lights blazed through the broken windows, and smoke poured from the stacks.

"Looks like we found our factory," Sam said.

Bling-bling!

Roger pointed his flashlight down a hole in the woods.

"And it looks like Roger found our way in," Mark said as he followed Roger down the hole.

"But . . . "

Sam spun around and held her metal fist in my face. I shut up and followed Mark down the tunnel. After a few minutes of tense silence, we got to a door. "Now what?" I asked, looking all over for a button or handle.

BOOF!

Sam punched a hole through the thin metal and walked inside. Mark and I took two steps through the door before gasping together once we saw inside. In a matter of hours, the robots had transformed an old and rusty paper mill into a state-of-the-art factory. Through a long window, we could see assembly lines that hadn't moved in decades whir away, spitting out part after part. Then there were these big claw arms putting parts together to make some of the robots we'd seen earlier in the game. Finally, all the way to the right hung an army of the walking robot suits that looked like the one Sam had been using at Bionosoft.

Sam pointed at the robot suits. "That's where we're headed."

We ducked into a tunnel at the far end of the window and crawled through. When Sam reached the end of the tunnel, she turned to us. "During this next part, it's VERY important that you do just as I say. Do you understand?"

We both nodded. Sam took a deep breath, looked up like she was rehearsing something in her head, and rolled out of the tunnel. Mark and I immediately followed. We emerged onto a moving assembly line surrounded by tight walls and a low ceiling. "Here! Now!" Sam yelled from up ahead. We ran to join her.

STAMP!

A metal part shook the assembly line as it stamped down right where Mark and I had been standing. Sam now had our full attention. "Three, two, one, JUMP!" she said.

We jumped. A saw blade came out of the wall, buzzing right where our feet had been. We didn't have time to rest, though, because Sam was already calling out the next command. "Roll!" We rolled under a metal beam. "Stay down!" Another buzz saw came out of the wall where our heads had been.

We continued the world's most dangerous game of Simon Says for the next few minutes until Sam shouted her last command, and we rolled off the assembly line. "Whew!" Sam looked exhilarated. "That was the first time I made it all the way through on one try!"

"WHAT?!"

Sam ignored me. "So there are the bot suits," she pointed across the room at the suits hanging a few feet off the ground, "and there are the guards," she pointed to a squadron of ninja-looking, knife-wielding robots standing in front of the suits.

"How do we get past them?" Mark asked.

"If you're really good with the boomerang, you can pick them off one by one as they run at you," Sam said.

I shook my head violently.

"The other way is sneaking through the ceiling."

After agreeing that the fewer boomerangs I needed to throw, the better, we all worked together to push boxes against the wall and use them as a staircase. Once we made it to the rafters, Sam turned, shushed us, then carefully started picking a path toward the armored suits.

About halfway there, Mark lifted his helmet visor and mouthed something to me. I am maybe the world's worst lip-reader, so, of course, I had no idea what he said. If I had to guess, maybe "Smelly watermelon baskets"? I nodded like I understood what he was talking about, which is what I usually do when I have no idea what the person is talking about. He kept staring at me for a response, which meant my tactic didn't work. Finally, I gave up and mouthed, "What?" He cupped his hand to his ear to signal for me to listen.

I stopped. It sounded like—a faint beeping? Is that what Mark was worried about? I shrugged and kept walking. With an army of knife-wielding death bots below us, a little beeping was the least of my worries.

But pretty soon, the beeping became one of those noises that you can't ignore once you hear it. I tried to focus on my next steps, but all I could concentrate on was the *beep-beep-beep*. I looked around again to try to locate it. It seemed to get louder the closer we got to our destination.

Beep-beep-beep.

I put my hand on a rafter to steady myself and felt a wire. I looked up to see that the wire led to a black box with a blinking red light. The box was stuck to the ceiling with Silly Putty or something. More wire connected that box to another box, which was strung to another one, which was connected to a . . . oh no!

Beep-beep-beep.

A quick look around the room revealed dozens of blinking black boxes all wired to a digital alarm clock near the bot suits. An alarm clock that was counting down from 37. I had seen enough movies to know what that looked like.

Beep-beep-beep.

Sam didn't seem concerned about the ticking, but I decided to ask her about it anyway, just to make sure it wasn't what it looked like. I quickly got Sam's attention. When she turned around, I mouthed, "Bomb?"

She nodded like she understood, but I could tell that she was doing the same thing I'd just done to Mark. I tried again. "Bomb!"

Beep-beep-beep.

She cocked her head and mouthed, "Mom?"

I looked back at the screen—28, 27, 26. No more fooling around. "BOMB!" I yelled while pointing at the clock.

The robots all looked up. Sam looked at the bomb, then back at me with panicked eyes. Yup. Definitely a bomb. "RUN!" she shouted. We bounded through the rafters as the knifebots followed below. Some of the robots worked together to climb to the rafters. I boomeranged one right before he could slice Mark from behind.

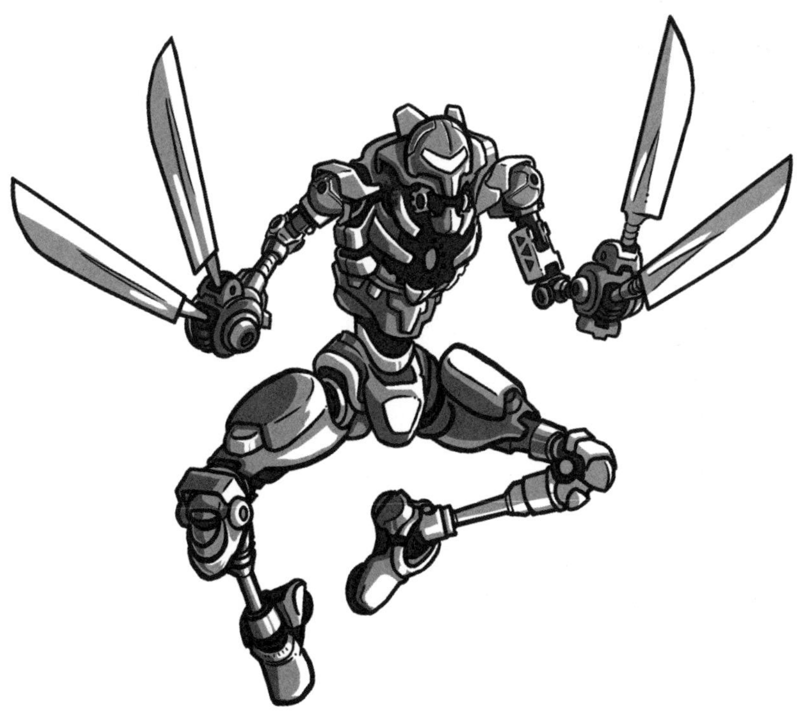

We made it to the robot suits hanging from the ceiling and swung down into them.

"Green button to start, pedals to move!" Sam shouted right before she closed a visor over her head. Her suit lit up, broke free from the rafters, and started sprinting away. Mark's robot joined her. I looked down at my control panel. Green button? What green button?! I peeked back up at the clock.

9. 8. 7.

Knifebots grabbed onto my robot skeleton's legs and started climbing. One dropped from the ceiling onto my robot's back.

6. 5.

I finally found the button.

4. 3.

While the visor lowered over my head, I desperately tried to find the pedals Sam had mentioned. Knifebots swarmed all over my suit. I could no longer see the timer, so I had to keep track in my head.

2.

The weight of all the robots broke the straps holding my suit, and we collapsed to the ground.

1.

Maybe if I—

BOOOOOOOOOOOOOOOM!

CHAPTER 14
Scrambled Eggs

I awoke to the feeling of an elephant standing on my chest. After trying and failing to move my arm a few times, I squinted to see that not an elephant but a stocky man in a suit had stepped on top of my robot armor. He was surveying the wreckage but didn't seem to notice me—probably because of all the debris covering my face. I quickly closed my eyes again.

"Nothing moving over here," he said in a deep tough-guy voice.

Another voice joined him. This one had a hint of a Southern accent. "That's it, then? Think that's the last of 'em?"

"Better be all the robots," Tough Guy said. "I've never seen command so worked up about anything in my life."

"What do you think is going on?"

"You know they don't tell us anything."

"Of course they don't tell us anything. I asked what you *think*."

Tough Guy paused for a second. Then his voice got low. "They had us doing memory resets on kids in the basement back there. *Kids!* Did you know that's the first time they've tried that on humans?"

"I—I had no idea."

"My hands were shaking the whole time. Thank goodness they all seemed to come through it fine, but if the agency is willing to risk turning kids' brains into scrambled eggs just to keep some secret—well, must be a pretty big secret."

"But what's the secret?"

"Don't you get it? With stuff like this, you don't ask questions, or YOUR brain gets turned into scrambled eggs. For real."

Southern Guy remained silent for a few seconds after that. Then he let out a soft, "Ohhhhh no."

"What?"

"Look."

I could feel a flashlight shining on my face. I held my breath and tried to keep perfectly still.

"That's one of the three that escaped, right?"

Tough Guy sighed. "Yeah," he said. "Hate to see that."

"Should we move the body, or . . . "

"Radio for backup and have the cleanup crew handle it," Tough Guy said. "They'll figure out a way to make it look like an accident or something. If this one is here, that means we've got to go through the rest of this mess to search for the others."

This time it was Southern Guy's turn to sigh. "I really hate this job sometimes," he said. Then they walked away.

I waited until I could no longer hear footsteps before daring to open my eyes again. The suits were gone. For that matter, so was the ceiling. I stared up at the moon through smoke and haze. I found that I couldn't move my head much at all in the suit, but I could move my eyes enough to see that I was surrounded by mountains of rubble, twisted metal, and robot parts.

I tried to wriggle out of my suit. Not only was I 100 percent stuck, but a bolt of pain shot through my leg whenever I tried moving. I stopped to catch my breath before trying again. Nothing. I was hungry and tired and hurting and wanted nothing more than to fall asleep right there. Maybe it wouldn't hurt if I closed my eyes for just a few secondssszzzzz . . .

NO.

I snapped my eyes back open and refocused. I was Eric's last chance. If I couldn't get out before the suits came back, he was gone for good. I took a few quick breaths, then sucked in my stomach and squirmed with all my might. My hip moved half an inch. I tried again. This time, my hip moved a whole inch! Progress! I squirmed some more until I was able to rock the suit back and forth with my hips. Back and forth, back and forth, and eventually, my body started moving inside the suit just a little on every "forth." For the next few minutes, I concentrated all my energy on rocking, then squirming, then finally a little bit of wriggling until—*POP!*—I freed my left hand from the robot. I flexed my fingers and rolled my hand a few times. Everything worked! I used that hand to pull out my other arm, and from there I used both hands to push my body out of the robot armor.

After I'd freed myself, I lay on the ground panting and sweating for a few seconds. Faraway flashlights cut through the smoke and darkness, but for now, I was alone. After I had a moment to catch my breath, I rolled over, pushed myself to my feet, and immediately fell back down.

I couldn't put an ounce of weight on the ankle I'd rolled earlier—it was completely broken. I looked back up at the flashlights. Two were getting closer. I quickly crawled behind a big piece of concrete and peeked out. The flashlights had turned left. I needed to put some distance between myself and the robot suit if I wanted any hope of making it out. I rolled underneath a collapsed sheet of metal, waited for two more flashlights to pass, then scrambled to an overturned conveyor belt. I continued that way across the smoldering heap of a factory until I had almost made it to the trees. I hopped behind another mangled robot armor and just started planning my final move to the forest when I felt something on my shoulder.

A tap.

I gasped and almost screamed, but the tapper quickly put a hand over my mouth. A cold metallic hand.

CHAPTER 15

BillyBotBoy

I slowly glanced out of the corner of my eye to see that I'd been discovered by Roger. He waved at me with his free claw, blinked his flashlight into the woods, and let me go. He then led me the rest of the way into the forest, where I found Sam and Mark huddled behind a big log. They were sitting next to Mark's helmet, which had cracked in two. Sam had a long gash across her forehead, and Mark had a homemade bandage wrapped around his upper arm, but otherwise they seemed OK.

Sam gave me a big hug and wouldn't let go. "You made it! You made it!" she kept repeating.

She started telling me about how she and Mark had miraculously escaped the blast, but I interrupted. "We need to move," I said and recounted the suits' conversation at the factory.

Sam and Mark seemed awed by the story. "Do you know who they are?" Mark asked.

I shrugged. "They mentioned 'the agency.' I don't know what that means, but I think they want to keep this whole thing a secret so they can use Mr. Gregory's technology for something down the road."

"So if they get to Eric before us . . . " Sam's voice trailed off.

"Scrambled eggs. Or worse."

"But it doesn't sound like they know the robots are building more levels, right?" Mark asked hopefully.

"Right. They didn't seem to know anything about who the robots are or what they're doing. They'll probably figure it out in the morning when people start reporting death bots everywhere, so that gives us a few hours to find Eric."

"We really need to skip ahead to the end of the game," Sam said.

"But how are we going to do that when we don't even know which direction to go?"

We thought in silence for a few moments. "What I wouldn't give for BillyBotBoy's number right now," Sam said.

"What's a BillyBotBoy?" Mark asked.

"He's an Aussie gamer who's obsessed with this game. He makes these brilliant *Super Bot World* videos," Sam said with a dreamy look in her eye.

A few more seconds of silence. Then Mark spoke up. "Are these videos on YouTube?"

"Of course," Sam said. "But I don't see a computer around here, do you?"

Mark remained quiet for a few more seconds. He seemed to be trying to decide whether to tell us something.

"What is it, Mark?" I asked.

"Well, we are actually pretty close to a computer," he said.

"Why didn't you say so?" Sam got up. "Let's go!"

Mark looked at me with a pained expression. "It's at my house."

I shook my head. "Mark . . . "

"We walk through my backyard, get the spare key, sneak into the basement, watch the video, and leave everything the way it was before my parents wake up." Mark said the whole thing in one sentence like he needed to get it all out before he could change his mind.

"Peaches," Sam said. Then she noticed me shaking my head. "What's the problem?"

"Mark has been in a video game for 80 years," I said.

"Eighty years?!"

Mark and I shushed her.

"Eighty years?!" Sam said quieter.

"Long story, but 80 years in video game time is almost two months in the real world," I said. "So by now, his parents think he's, uh—well, they think he's dead."

"So he can't just go bopping into his house at two in the morning, can he?" Sam said.

"Right," I said. "If we wake up his parents, we're never getting back out of the house to rescue Eric."

Sam nodded, seeing the big picture now. "But if we don't wake them up, then Mark will have to leave the house without knowing for sure that he'll ever get to see them again."

We both looked at Mark. He turned around and started walking through the woods.

"Come back here!" Sam hissed.

He spun around. "Stop wasting time!" Without waiting for an argument, he turned and started walking again. Sam and Roger quickly followed.

"Hey, guys," I said, still on the ground. "Bad news—I can't really walk anymore."

"Oh my!" Sam said. She and Mark came back, helped me to my feet, and supported my weight all the way to Mark's house. He was right—it was close. After 15 minutes of navigating through the woods, Mark shushed us, and we turned into a backyard. We crept through the yard and then nearly jumped out of our skin when a motion-sensor light turned on. Mark shook his head and hurried to the back patio, grabbed a fake rock from the garden, unscrewed it, then pulled out a key. He quickly got us all into the house, then shut the door behind him.

Once we made it inside, we stopped for a few seconds to rest. The house was dark and silent except for the hum of the refrigerator. When my eyes readjusted to the darkness, I saw that we were standing right next to the kitchen table, where Mark's parents still had a place set for him. I glanced over at Mark to see how he was doing. He kept his eyes focused on the ground. He'd probably spent the past 80 years dreaming of this moment, and he couldn't even let himself enjoy it because he knew he had to turn right back around. After we caught our breath, he motioned for us to follow him into the basement.

Mark's basement looked like it had been a fun place at one time. But now wilting flower arrangements from the memorial service covered the Ping-Pong table, the big portrait from our school's "Mark Day" stood between a movie projector and "theater screen" wall, and every trophy Mark had ever won cluttered the overstuffed couch. Roger lit the way as we quietly navigated through all the memories of Mark. Again, Mark refused to look at any of it.

"You OK?" I whispered.

Mark sat down at the computer. "I'm fine," he said, but he said it real fast, in that way you do when you're on the verge of tears but don't want to give it away. He turned on the monitor and stared at it with a funny expression on his face.

"What's wrong?" Sam whispered.

"I can't remember the password."

"You can't remember?!"

"It's been 80 years! Just give me a second." Mark finally nodded and typed something.

USERNAME OR PASSWORD INCORRECT

He furrowed his eyebrows and tried again.

USERNAME OR PASSWORD INCORRECT

"I know that was it," he muttered. He tried again. Same result.

"Maybe they changed it," I said. I looked around the room and got an idea. I reached over and typed "Mark."

USERNAME OR PASSWORD INCORRECT

"Wait a second," Mark said. He typed, "M@rk1."

WELCOME

Mark smiled. "My dad always replaced the 'a's with '@'s and added a '1' to the end of all his passwords. He thought it was more secure."

"Thinks," Sam said.

"Huh?"

"He *thinks* it's more secure," Sam said. "He's still alive."

"Yeah," Mark said. "Yeah, I guess he is." He turned back to the computer and started YouTube. "All you, Sam."

Sam pulled up a video titled "Super Bot World 3 Playthrough—EPIC Finale! (Part 17/17)."

"G'DAY EVERYONE!" a boisterous BillyBotBoy yelled from the speakers. "TODAY, WE'RE GONNA GET THIS CHEEKY FELLA TO HIS PRINCESS, BUT FIRST . . . "

Mark jumped across the desk to hit the mute button. Sam paused the video, and we waited for a full minute without breathing to listen for any movement upstairs. Fortunately, Mark's parents were heavy sleepers.

Sam pressed play again. A robot decked out with Sam's metal fist as well as 30 other upgrades ran onto the screen. A few seconds later, Roger flew in behind him.

Bleep-bloooooooooop.

We all turned in a panic to shush the real Roger, but something was wrong. Seeing himself on the computer screen seemed to cause a short circuit in his brain.

Bloooowoooorooooop.

He wobbled and swayed midair while making loud, dying-computer noises. Sam grabbed a box of Mark memories from the desk, dumped it out, and used it to cover Roger. That finally shut him up.

"What was that?" Mark hissed to Sam.

She shrugged and shook her head with wide eyes. We waited for any sign of Mark's parents again, then turned back to the screen.

The character seemed to be floating through a futuristic hallway. He was a blur of motion, dodging fireballs, kicking off walls, and mowing through enemies. Finally, he got to a big metal switch on the wall and flipped it. Gravity came back on, and everything fell to the ground.

"It's some sort of antigravity chamber, I guess?" Mark said. "Where would you even find an antigravity chamber?!"

But then the character walked into the next room, and we discovered exactly where someone might find an antigravity chamber. In this new room, the entire back wall was a window. And through that window, way in the distance, was planet Earth.

CHAPTER 16
Lavers Hill

"THE MOON?! I CAN'T GO TO THE MOON!" Sam started screaming while whispering at the same time, which is kind of a hard thing to do. "I DON'T KNOW ANYTHING ABOUT THE MOON! I MEAN, I KNOW YOU CAN'T BREATHE! HOW WOULD WE BREATHE ON THE MOON? HOW WOULD WE GET OFF THE MOON?!"

"Sam!" I interrupted. "Relax! If they make it to the moon, it's too late for Eric anyway."

Sam took a second to breathe. Mark was already scrolling through the other videos. "Here's the level that comes before the moon one," he said.

We watched the main character fight an enormous boss in front of a rocket preparing for blastoff. They battled on an open field in the middle of farm country. I wrinkled my nose. "A farm? Really? Seems like a pretty boring place to put a level."

"It's Lavers Hill," Sam said.

"Excuse me?"

"Lavers Hill. It's the hometown of the guy who created *Super Bot World.* He always puts it in his games."

"And I'm assuming that's in Australia?" Mark said.

"Sure is."

"Great." Mark leaned back in his chair. "So instead of going to the moon, we need to go to Australia."

"I don't think so," I said. "Look, it's just farms and fields. As long as the robots find something like that near us, they'll build their level here."

"We're in Ohio," Mark said. "The whole state is farms and fields."

I wasn't about to lose hope yet. "They seem to keep the levels close to each other. Maybe we can figure out where they're building the other levels and map out a path."

With no other options, Mark sneaked to the garage and came back a few minutes later with a big paper map. "My dad always kept a paper map in the car," he explained. Then he looked at Sam and corrected himself. "I mean 'keeps.' He *keeps* a map in the car."

Mark unfolded the map on the desk and studied it for a few seconds. "OK, Bionosoft is here," he drew a circle on the map. "The paper mill is here," he drew another circle. "Now let's find Level Four." He played another BillyBotBoy video. This one showed the robot hero launching a rocket-powered hovercraft off the first hill of a roller coaster.

"Kiddie Park?" I guessed.

Mark circled it on his map.

Sam shook her head. "A theme park for cats? What is wrong with America?"

"Not *Kitty* Park," I said. "*Kiddie* Park. It's an amusement park in our town just for little kids."

Sam had tuned out before I'd finished my explanation, so it's entirely possible that she still thinks America is a land full of amusement parks for cats. She'd already moved on to the video of the next level. "Looks like it's pirate themed?" she said.

I nodded. "Kiddie Park is next to Lake Erie, so that makes sense."

By 3 a.m., we'd circled locations for every level in the game and connected them all with a line. Sam stepped back, stared at the map for a moment, and then said what we were all thinking. "Well, that looks like a whole heap of nothing."

"It does kind of follow a pattern," I pointed out. "Like a swirl or a swoop or, uh, a curlicue."

"Whatever it is, it ends up in the middle of nowhere," Mark said.

"Just pull up the satellite view of that area," I said.

Mark did—there were farms everywhere.

"Boom!" I said. Then I noticed something. "Zoom in on that road."

Buildings came into focus. Google Maps started putting names over businesses. Holmes County Seed and Feed. Yoder Meats. Berlin Farmstead Dutch Kitchen. "I know this place," I said excitedly. "It's Amish country!"

Sam looked at me weird.

"Amish country!" I repeated. "You don't have that in Australia?"

"Is this another cat thing?"

"The Amish don't believe in electricity, so they mostly work on farms and make things out of wood and sell pies and stuff. Anyways, the important thing is if the robots are building a giant rocket ship in Amish country, we'll see it from miles away!"

"There's just one problem," Mark said. "Look." He'd mapped out the walking route from his house to Amish country: 22 hours and 15 minutes. We stared at that number in silence for a few seconds; then I clicked back to the rocket-powered roller-coaster video from earlier. An idea had started forming in my head.

"We've been playing by the robots' rules this whole time, right?" I asked.

Sam and Mark shrugged.

"Maybe it's time we make up our own rules."

CHAPTER 17
Kiddie Park

After a half hour of watching videos, making plans, and gathering supplies, we were ready. Mark shut off the computer and lifted the box off of Roger. "Come on, buddy. We're going to need you."

Beep, Roger replied, using his quietest setting.

Before Mark could get out of the chair, Sam put her hand on his shoulder. "Mark," she said. That was as far as she got before Mark interrupted her.

"Look, I know you're going to give some big speech about why I need to stay. And, believe me, I want nothing more than to go upstairs right now, curl up in my own bed, and then eat my mom's banana-chocolate-chunk pancakes in the morning. But that's not what we do. That's not what you did, that's not what Jesse did, and that's certainly not what Eric did. We stick together and help each other no matter what. So if there's even a tiny chance I can still help Eric, there's nothing you can say that will stop me from trying. Got it?"

Sam stared at him for a second before finally finishing her sentence. "I was just going to remind you to bring the map."

Mark's face turned red. "Oh. Got it." He stuffed the map in his book bag and led us out of the house to the garage. We squeezed past a red minivan and pulled out the bikes. Sam grabbed Mark's mom's bicycle, Mark got his own, and—since I still couldn't walk—I climbed onto Mark's handlebars. We silently pedaled through town until Kiddie Park came into view. Actually, I should probably just call it "Park," because there was no longer anything "Kiddie" about it. Overnight, the robots had transformed the cute merry-go-round into a whirling death machine. The choo choo train tracks that circled the park now disappeared underground where, I'm sure, terrifying robots were waiting. And the Little Dipper, which was a disappointing thrill ride even when I was six years old, had a new 150-foot hill.

We dumped our bikes next to the front gate and put our plan into motion. "Don't screw this up, Roger," Sam said.

Beep-beep!

Roger flew through the entrance of the park while we circled back near the Little Dipper. We waited until we heard Roger start his distraction (whistling "Kookaburra Sits in the Old Gum Tree" as obnoxiously as possible over and over) and then hopped the fence. Well, technically Sam and Mark hopped the fence. I tried twice before Sam finally ripped the fence apart with her metal hand. All three of us piled into the roller-coaster hovercraft and pulled down the safety harnesses. Mark flipped a switch, cracked his knuckles, and turned to smile at us. Then he pushed the throttle forward ever so slightly.

WHOOMF!

That little bit of throttle rocketed us to 100 miles per hour in about two seconds. We shot up the hill and launched into the night sky.

"AHHHHH!"

I screamed, not only because flying off of roller-coaster tracks is my worst nightmare but also because we'd just watched a robot dragon pluck BillyBotBoy's character out of the sky and carry him to the fun house of terror at this exact point in the game.

WHOOSH!

The robot dragon arrived a half second too late and flew right past our hovercraft. He shrieked and shook his head as he zoomed past us, probably trying to get rid of the annoying whistling drone that was blocking his vision. As soon as the dragon passed by, Roger zipped into our vehicle.

"Nice job!" Mark yelled.

Beepbeepbeepbeep-beep-booooooop!

THUMP!

We finally landed on the ground and steered toward Kiddie Park's front gate.

"SCREEECH!"

The robot dragon hit the ground behind us and blasted fire in our direction. Mark dodged the blast, pushed the throttle forward, and zoomed out of the park faster than a Formula One race car driver. Decades of mastering the hover tank in *Full Blast* had given Mark almost superhuman reflexes in the driver's seat, and he needed every ounce of that ability to navigate the twisty residential streets outside of Kiddie Park. If the suits didn't know about the other robots by now, the clock had certainly started ticking, as a metallic dragon chasing a speeding hovercraft isn't something you see outside your house every day. Mark followed the route we'd plotted in his basement and ended up at Columbia Beach Park in less than a minute. He flew past the playground and launched off the pier.

Once we made it to the water, Sam turned around. "I think we lost the dragon."

"SCREEEECH!"

A fire blast lit up the lake as the dragon swooped down. Mark yanked the wheel hard right, throwing up a huge wake of water. The dragon pulled back up and pursued from above as we skipped across Lake Erie.

"SCREE—"

BOOM!

A cannonball stopped the dragon mid-screech.

BOOMBOOMBOOM!

Mark got low as he navigated through the cannonballs splashing all around us. We approached the dark shape of a massive pirate ship. Suddenly—*WHOOSH!*—the slain dragon landed in the water behind us and produced a wave big enough to launch us onto the ship's deck.

"It's over there!" Sam shouted, pointing at the mast. Mark drove through an army of robot skeleton pirates toward a glowing cube. "This one's yours, Jesse!" Sam said.

I reached out just far enough to touch the button on top of the cube as we passed by.

ZZZZZING!

The cube transformed into a million metal pieces that slid down my body and reassembled themselves into robot legs. I rotated my right ankle in a circle. "It works now!" I exclaimed.

"Good!" Mark shouted as he flew off the back plank. We sped up the coast until we reached another level in Ohio's only drive-through safari. Mark surprised a robot lion by driving into its den. He snatched a power-up cube that gave him an Iron Man blaster hand, then pushed the throttle to blow past a pride of real lions before they had a chance to react. As we were leaving the safari, a metal giraffe started galloping behind us and extending its head with an Inspector Gadget neck. Mark turned around to fire his new blaster, but Sam punched the giraffe with her metal fist before he could get a chance.

"Eyes on the road!" she yelled.

We zoomed toward Alpine Snow Trails ski resort. The resort didn't quite have the majestic peaks of the video game's snow level, but the robots had managed to create an impressive amount of fake snow for the beginning of May. Mark sped up the slope and dodged an abominable snow monster so Sam could snag one of the most boring power-ups in the game—a portable battery pack. With that final piece of the puzzle, we merged onto I-77 toward Amish country. Since there were very few cars on the road at 5 a.m., Mark could really open up the throttle.

After a few minutes of weaving in and out of traffic at blistering speeds, a police siren turned on behind us. My shoulders slumped. I was afraid of this. I couldn't imagine that the police would look too kindly on a 12-year-old without a license driving at 200 miles per hour.

“Go faster,” Sam said. “They can’t keep up.”

“We don’t do that in America!” I blurted out, slightly less comfortable with a high-speed police chase than Sam appeared to be. “We should at least talk to them, right? Maybe they can help us! Maybe . . . ”

My voice trailed off as I watched the police car start catching up to us. We were traveling at speeds impossible without rocket assistance. When did the highway patrol get jet-cars? As if to answer my question, a head emerged from the passenger window. The red and blue lights illuminated the guy’s clothing, and even in the predawn darkness, I could tell he didn’t have a police uniform.

He was wearing a suit.

CHAPTER 18
Goliatron

The suit hanging out of the window pulled out something long and rifle-like.

CRACK!

It was, in fact, a rifle.

“Turn off the road!” Sam yelled.

Mark made a hard right directly into a cornfield.

THWACK-THWACK-THWACK-THWACK.

We all covered our faces as the hovercraft tore a path through the cornstalks. After a few seconds of driving blind, the thwacking stopped, and we found ourselves in an open field. Or at least it was mostly open.

“COW!” Sam screamed.

Mark yanked the steering wheel right to dodge a cow.

“SHEEP!”

Mark weaved left to dodge the sheep.

"DUCK!"

"WHERE?!" Mark yelled. "I DON'T SEE A . . . "

Sam yanked Mark down with her as she ducked a millisecond before we passed underneath the blade of a threshing machine.

Mark popped back up just in time to see the fence in front of us. "Whoa!" He yanked the steering wheel, but it was too late. We barreled into the fence at 200 miles per hour. The fence snapped from its post and tangled around us as we bounced across the field. I squeezed my eyes shut and held onto the safety harness until we rolled to a stop.

When everything settled, I peeked my eyes open to see Mark with his head in his hands.

"You OK?" I asked.

"I'm fine," he said. "But how are we gonna find Eric now?"

"Look up."

Just across the field, silhouetted against the rising sun, was a 150-foot-tall rocket ship. Dozens of robots scurried up and down a stair tower that reached all the way to the rocket's cone. And next to the stair tower, standing almost as tall as the rocket, was Goliatron.

Gulp.

Of all the scary video game creatures I'd stared down over the past 24 hours, none was scarier than the boss of Lavers Hill. I had known what was coming thanks to the BillyBotBoy video, but in person—wow. While I stared at the robot, Sam jumped out of the hovercraft and started running left.

"Do you see it?!" Mark shouted to Sam.

"It should be next to the barn," she said without turning around.

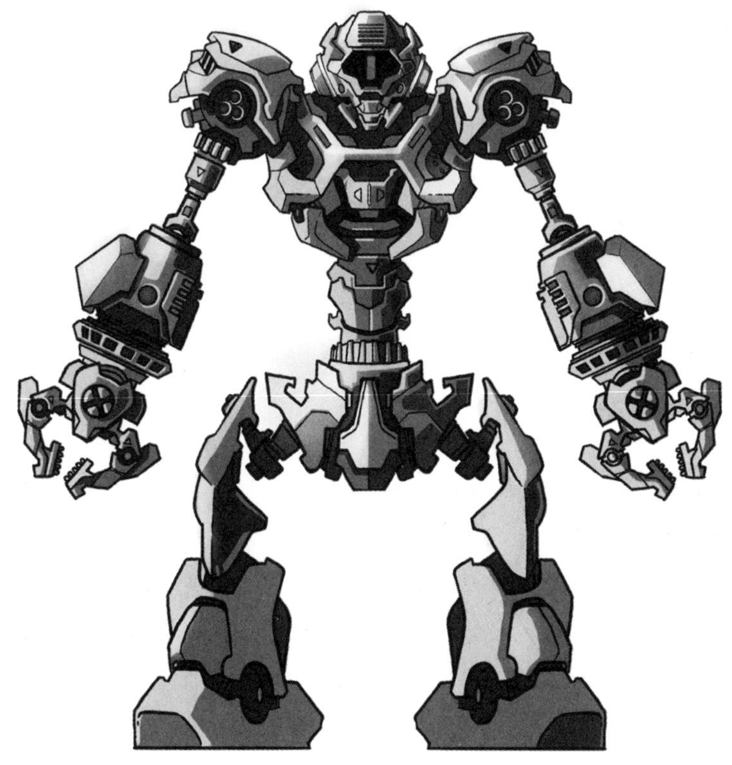

Mark took a few steps toward the barn before realizing I hadn't yet left the hovercraft. He ran back and grabbed my shoulder. "Jesse." He looked me in the eye. "You got this, OK? Remember—distract and stall." He patted my shoulder and ran toward Sam. "Did you find it yet?!"

"Distract and stall" sounded a lot better from the safety of Mark's basement than it did staring at a 12-story robot whose only goal was to pound me into the ground. Goliatron noticed Mark first and started walking toward him. That kicked me into action. "Hey!" I yelled. The robot spun around and glared at me. "Come on!" I said, trying to sound tough. "Let's rumble!"

Let's rumble? I was so bad at video game smack talk.

Goliatron pounded his fists together a few times like a boxer and started lumbering toward me. I looked around in a panic. Where was Roger? He was supposed to be my distract-and-stall buddy! *Ting!* Something hit Goliatron in the back of the head. He paused, shook his head, then continued walking toward me. *Tingtingting!* It was Roger! The little drone was battling a robot 100 times his size by running into the back of its head over and over. Goliatron turned around to find the distraction, which gave me enough time to throw a boomerang.

Clank!

It hit him right in the chest. It wasn't enough to hurt him, of course, but it did make him turn back toward me.

Ting!

Roger got him again.

Clank!

Then I did. I glanced nervously toward the barn—this couldn't last for long. "How are you guys doing over there?" I called out.

"Found it!" Mark grabbed the power-up cube he and Sam had been trying to find.

Ting!

Mark ran toward the rocket while stuffing the cube in his book bag, being careful not to press the button. "You're doing great!"

Clank!

"I'm almost ready, too!" Sam shouted.

Ting!

"Keep it up!" she said.

THWACK!

That "THWACK" was neither Roger nor me. It was Goliatron, who'd finally been able to swat Roger out of the air. Roger spun and tumbled 12 stories.

"ROGER! NOOOO!" I screamed.

CRACK!

Roger split in half when he hit the ground. He then bounced a few more times, leaving a trail of broken plastic behind.

I stared at my little buddy in shock. Then Goliatron turned back to me, his eyes glowing red. I backed up. He started marching toward me with a purpose, the ground rumbling with every step.

"Sam?" I yelled over my shoulder. "Ready yet?!"

No answer. The robot got closer.

"Sam?!"

I threw the boomerang again. It didn't even faze him. Each step was now shaking the ground so much that I couldn't move. "SAM?!"

"HEY YOU BIG DUFFER!" Sam finally screamed.

Both Goliatron and I turned to Sam. She had rigged the laptop and projector from Mark's house to the battery pack from the ski resort. "Check this out!" She pressed a button on the keyboard, and suddenly BillyBotBoy's Lavers Hill video projected onto the barn. The robot tilted its head, confused. Sam clicked "play," and Goliatron stared at his character in the game. I watched his reaction closely. If this didn't work, we were done. There was no plan B.

Goliatron did nothing but stare for a few seconds. Come on, come on, come on. Then I noticed his hand start trembling. Good. I could see him trying to pivot toward me, but something about the video made it impossible for him to turn away.

"Turn up the sound!" I yelled.

Sam turned it up just as the video Goliatron let out a loud roar. When real-life Goliatron heard it, he began making that dying robot noise that Roger had made when he saw himself on video. "Louder!"

Sam cranked the volume as loud as it would go. Goliatron stumbled backward, visibly shaking all over now. His legs wobbled, then his head twitched. Just like Roger, his microchip brain couldn't seem to process seeing himself in a video game. Then, without warning—

BOOM!

He exploded. I curled into a ball to protect myself as millions of hot metal shards showered onto the field. When it was finally over, I looked around. With Goliatron gone, all the other robots had made a beeline for the rocket ship. Ready or not, they were taking off.

I scanned the stair tower and found Mark about halfway up. He was using his Iron Man hand like a pro, blasting, punching, and chopping his way through a horde of bad guys. I followed the stair tower up to the open door in the cone. We'd come all this way assuming that Eric was inside that door, but what if he wasn't? What if they'd already . . .

A head poked out of the door for just a second before getting pulled back in. "ERIC!" I yelled.

The head poked back out again. "Jesse?!" Eric yelled before getting yanked back in. He struggled his way back to the door. "Did you see the robot monster out there?! IT'S HU . . ." Yank. He reappeared another second later. "And the robot pirates? Did you know they have robot pirates?!"

"Eric, don't worry, we're . . . "

Yank. I waited for him to come to the door again. "Mark is coming to get . . . "

Eric interrupted me. "Mark is here?! You guys should come check out this rocket! It's incredible!"

"It's going to the moon!" I yelled.

Eric fought off another robot that was grabbing for him. "What?!"

"IT'S GOING TO THE MOON!"

This was news to Eric. He started to panic. "I CAN'T LIVE ON THE MOON!"

"Mark's almost there!"

By now, Mark was just one flight of stairs away from Eric. He pulled the power-up out of his bag and held his finger over the button. This particular power-up was a heavily armored hot-air balloon that you were supposed to use to get eye level with Goliatron so you could hit the weak spot on his forehead. The plan was for Mark to press the button just as he reached Eric, drag him into the balloon, and land safely in the field as the rocket took off. It was not the most thorough plan—none of us knew the first thing about flying a hot-air balloon, for example—but it had been the best we could do at 3 a.m.

"Eric!" Mark said as he ran up the last set of stairs. "When I press the button . . . "

KAPOW!

An explosion rocked the stair tower, knocking Mark off his feet and causing him to drop the power-up cube over the side. I heard a click to my right and looked over to see a suit standing behind the super-powered police car from earlier. He aimed a rocket launcher and fired another shot.

KAPOW!

This one exploded almost exactly where the first one had. The entire stair tower groaned, leaned, groaned some more, and then finally toppled, taking Mark with it.

CHAPTER 19
The Rocket

Before I could process what had happened, my legs started moving. I was at least 70 yards away from the rocket—way too far to do anything except scream—but I ran anyway. And when I took my first step, I got a surprise. I was fast. Really fast. Like superhero fast. I pushed off with one of my robot legs and launched five feet forward. I took another step and bounded another 10 feet. I ran at the rocket with all my might. Usually in the movies, these scenes happen in slow motion. It's almost as if the hero is moving so fast that everything else seems to pause around him.

That would have been nice.

Instead, time sped up. I made it to the rocket in less than two seconds, and—bad news—two seconds is not nearly enough time to come up with a plan. Without a plan, I covered my head as metal crashed around me.

CLUNK!

The cube Mark had dropped landed at my feet. I pressed the button, and it instantly *POOF*ed into a humongous hot-air balloon. I hopped into the basket and curled up while the crashing continued. This was when time slowed down. Every clang and every crash felt like it was going to be the one to rip through the balloon and nail me to the ground. Finally, there was one last huge *CRASH* and everything stopped.

After a few seconds of silence, I heard rustling above me. I poked my head out. “Mark?!” An arm flopped over the edge of the half-deflated balloon. “Mark!” The arm went back. I climbed out of the basket as fast as I could and looked up. The stair tower lay in a mangled mess over the balloon. Blown-up robot parts littered the ground.

PLOP.

Something rolled off the side of the balloon. I ran around to investigate.

“Mark!” I yelled when I saw him lying on the ground. “Are you OK?”

He rolled over to face me. His face was completely black from the blast, and his Iron Man hand looked partially melted. “Listen, Jesse. They’re gonna . . . ” He struggled to his feet. “They’re gonna . . . ”

At that moment, a hand grabbed the back of my shirt.

"Run!" I yelled.

But Mark couldn't run, because another suit had grabbed him, too. Mark struggled against his captor. Even though he'd just nearly died from both an explosion and a 15-story fall, he kicked and flailed and fought harder than I'd ever seen him fight before. He managed to tear the guy's suit coat off his back, but that was as far as he got before the man wrangled both of Mark's hands behind his back and started dragging him across the field. My suit joined him, and we soon met up with two other suits who'd captured Sam.

"You got the memory wipe, Doug?" my suit said to one of Sam's guards.

Doug shook his head. "Can't use it on them," he said. "This is the one who's been missing for a month." He nodded at Mark.

"Are you kidding? So what do we do with them, then?"

"You've still got one rocket left, right?" he asked.

The guy holding me looked at the rocket launcher strapped to his back. "Aw, come on, I can't do that," he said.

“He’s been gone for a month,” Doug said. “You know there’ll be questions if we send him back out, even with the memory wipe.”

“But can’t we just bring him in?”

“Orders are orders. Now tie them up, and let’s get it over with.”

I looked around in a panic. Sam, who usually had something tough to say, slumped against her captor in defeat.

“Wait!” Mark said. “There’s one more!”

“One more kid?” Doug asked. “Sorry, we’ve got them all.”

“Eric. His name is Eric Conrad. He wasn’t in a video game, so he’s not in your records. He’s still out here. If you don’t believe me, just ask Mr. Gregory.”

The suits looked at each other, and Doug stepped up to Mark. “OK, kid. Where is he?”

“I’m not telling until you let them go.”

Doug looked down at Mark’s black face and gnarled metal hand. “I don’t think you’re in a position to negotiate.”

“Come on,” Mark said. “Just do the memory wipe or whatever and let them go. I’m the only one you need to get rid of.”

“Yeah, Doug,” one of the suits chimed in. “Why don’t we just do that?”

Doug spun around. “You think command is playing around?!” he yelled. “If we don’t clean this up, we’re the ones who are going to disappear! Do you understand that? Do you?!”

Before the other suit could answer, he got interrupted by an earth-shaking, chest-vibrating roar. We all spun around to see smoke pouring from the bottom of the rocket.

"WAIT!" I screamed. "NO! STOP! WE HAVE TO STOP IT!"

Nobody moved to stop anything. The roar got louder, and the smoke got thicker until the rocket blasted off with Eric inside.

CHAPTER 20

3, 2, 1 . . .

"NO!" I screamed at the rocket. "ERIC, NO!" I continued yelling at the rocket as it disappeared above the clouds. Then I collapsed on the ground and started crying in front of everyone. I'd lost my best friend.

Doug's voice got soft. "I'm sorry," he said.

I continued crying without looking up. "Just do whatever it is you're going to do."

Without saying a word, one of the suits produced a rope and tied us all up. It went fast—none of us had the strength to struggle anymore. When he finished the job, he pushed us together with our backs facing each other.

"Just close your eyes," Doug said as he loaded up the rocket launcher. "This will all be over soon."

I squeezed my eyes closed.

"3. 2. 1."

BOOM!

I felt the heat and shockwave of the blast but no pain. Had he missed? I opened my eyes to see the suits scrambling for cover. Then I noticed that their vehicle had been blown to bits.

"What was that?!" Doug yelled. "Did anybody see where that came from?!"

Nobody had time to answer because a sheriff's car screamed up the gravel road at that moment. Two deputies jumped out. "Drop your weapons!" one of them shouted.

The suits looked at each other, trying to decide whether they should fight back. Three more sheriff's cars pulled up. "DROP THEM!" another man said.

The suits dropped their weapons and put their hands behind their heads. The officers ran over and cuffed them. "Are you kids OK?" one of the officers asked as he untied us. I didn't answer because I was staring at the hot-air balloon. One of the cannons was smoking as if it had just been fired. But how? Just then, a head popped up. No . . . it couldn't be.

"Eric?"

"That. Was. AWESOME!" Eric yelled as he climbed out of the basket and started running toward us. "DID YOU GUYS SEE THAT CAR?!"

"Why did you wait so long to shoot?!" Mark asked. "He was on 1!"

"Eric?" I still couldn't get over the fact that my friend was running toward us instead of rocketing to the moon.

Eric reached us and started helping the officer with the knots. "You said to wait until the last second," he said.

"He was on 1!" Mark repeated. "He was going to shoot on 0!"

"Yeah," Eric said. "That's the definition of the last second."

"Can someone please tell me what's going on?!" I asked.

Mark and Eric had to explain the whole thing three times before I finally understood. According to them, Eric had seen the hot-air balloon inflate from the rocket, decided it was his only chance to escape, and jumped. Both he and Mark landed safely on the half-inflated balloon and came up with a quick plan together. Mark would roll off the balloon and give himself up. Then, when a suit would grab him, he'd struggle and flail like he was trying to get away, but really, he'd steal the suit's phone out of his pocket and throw it up to Eric, who was still hiding on top of the hot-air balloon. Eric would call 911, then sneak off the balloon, crawl into the basket, and blast the suits' car to keep them from driving away when the police came.

"OK, I think I understand everything," I said. "But I just have one more question. WHY DID YOU WAIT SO LONG TO SHOOT?!"

Eric tried to explain his reasoning again, but I got distracted by Sam, who bumped me as she gestured wildly while talking on the phone.

"Yes, Mum, Amish country," she said. "It's an American thing. I don't know; it's like Lavers Hill. You know Lavers Hill? Look, I'm sure it's on the telly by now. Turn it on and see for yourself. There are loads of cameras everywhere."

She was right. It seemed like every news station in the country had descended on the Amish farm, and the crowd was growing by the minute. Everyone kept trying to talk to us, but the sheriff's office pushed all the cameras away. Finally, a black car pulled up, and a familiar porcupine-haired man stepped out from the back seat.

"Mr. Gregory!" I shouted.

The deputies stepped aside as Mr. Gregory ran to us. "I can't believe it!" he said with a huge smile. "You all made it!"

"You wouldn't believe everything that happened!" I said. "There was this mine cart and roller-coaster hovercraft and a drone named Roger . . ." my voice trailed off as I remembered Roger.

Mr. Gregory took my pause as an opportunity to jump in. "I have a very important question for all of you right now." He lowered his voice. "Have any of you said anything about The Agency?"

We all looked at each other confused. "The Agency?" Mark asked.

"Yes, the men in suits."

We looked even more confused. "I guess not," I said.

"Good." Mr. Gregory got serious. "Don't. Just trust me."

Before we could ask any follow-up questions, a red minivan squealed to a stop next to the ambulance—the same red minivan we'd seen in Mark's garage earlier that morning.

Because Mark looked just like us, it was easy to forget that he'd already lived a full lifetime inside of a video game. He'd already been a kid, a teenager, an adult, and finally an old man—and he'd spent every one of those days dreaming about a single moment.

Before Mark's dad could shut off the car, his mom had jumped out. "Mark!" she screamed with tears in her eyes.

Mark just sat there with his feet dangling out of the back of the ambulance and the biggest smile on his face, soaking in every little thing about this moment. He was finally home.

CHAPTER 21
Mark Day II

I spent nearly every second of the next two weeks with Eric. We told our story over and over to police, to reporters, to friends, and mostly to each other. We'd be sitting in Eric's room, and he'd smirk and say something like, "Remember the look on your face when I pushed you off that waterfall?"

Then I'd come back with something like, "No, but I do remember watching you scream like a girl when those fur balls attacked."

"They had razors for teeth!"

"I dunno, they looked pretty harmless to me."

It was good to have my best friend back.

One thing we didn't talk about—with anyone—was "The Agency." Thanks to testimony from us and Mr. Gregory, Bionosoft had been shut down for good. Jevvrey Delfino and everyone who'd worked together to trap kids in video games had been put in jail for a very long time. But nobody knew what to do with the suits. They wouldn't talk, and neither would we. The four that had been captured stayed in jail, but since they all had fake IDs, police never figured out their identity or their employer.

The weeks went by in a parade of interviews and parties and actual parades. But my favorite event was Mark Day II, on the last day of school. Since our school had held a "Mark Day" back when they thought Mark was gone for good, they decided they needed to do something special to celebrate his coming back from the dead. There were balloons and pizzas and speeches from me, Eric, and even Sam by video conference. We got her to do her American accent, which was a big hit with the school. After I finished my speech, I hobbled back to my seat on stage (only one more week with the cast! Woo-hoo!), and Mark got up.

We were all worried about how he'd handle his first few months back in the real world, but he was doing great so far. The doctors had managed to get the gnarled Iron Man hand off his arm and put his real hand back together good as new. All the teachers had been helping him relearn everything he'd forgotten from his time in the video game so he could graduate to seventh grade with the rest of our class. The state of Ohio was even considering giving him an honorary driver's license to commemorate his legendary hovercraft run. When he got to the podium, Mark waved, said a few sentences about how grateful he was for all the nice things everyone had done for him, and sat back down 20 seconds later, his face a little red from embarrassment.

Then Principal Ortega got up to close the ceremony. "Before we go, we have one more surprise for our heroes," she said with a smile. With that, she gave way to Mr. Gregory, who arrived on stage with a big box in his hands.

Mr. Gregory waved to the crowd and turned to us. "We could never do enough to thank you boys for your bravery," he said. "But I've been working on something for the past two weeks to show my personal gratitude for all you've done. Can we bring Sam back, please?"

Sam reappeared on the big screen behind Mr. Gregory. "What is this?" she asked.

"You should have received a package in the mail today," Mr. Gregory said. "I want you to open it at the same time we open ours on stage, OK?"

"OK . . . "

"Three, two, one!"

Beep-beep-boooooooooooop!

Roger flew out of the box and did a triple flip in the air. At the same time, an identical Roger flew out of Sam's box.

"NOOOOOOOO!" she screamed.

"Meet the original Roger, remade with 82 percent original parts," Mr. Gregory said as he gestured to the Roger on stage. Then he turned to Sam. "And Roger II, a perfect replica of everyone's favorite robot friend."

"NOOOOOOOO!" Sam continued.

I jumped from my chair. "No way!" Roger spun around and gave me a high five.

"And that's all for today!" Principal Ortega said. "Have a safe summer, everyone!"

Eric, Mark, and I gathered around Mr. Gregory and thanked him over and over, while Roger zoomed around us, whistling merrily. At some point during the celebration, I noticed Mr. Gregory's son Charlie standing off to the side. When I made eye contact with him, he made a slight "come here" motion with his head. I excused myself from the group. "What's up?" I asked.

Charlie looked around and silently walked into the locker room. I followed. Inside the locker room, he checked out every nook and cranny, then turned on one of the showers.

"What are you doing?" I asked.

He motioned for me to shush while he turned on two more showers. Finally, he huddled in close. "I'm making noise in case they have listening devices in here. I saw it on TV once."

"Listening devices? Who has listening devices?!"

Charlie ignored the question. "Have you noticed anything weird about my dad lately?"

"Weird? Like what? I haven't seen him much since the robots."

"I don't know. Weird. Like anything out of the ordinary."

I didn't know what Charlie was trying to get at. "Charlie, I barely know your dad. He helped us rescue Mark, but to be honest, he was a little weird then, too," I said with a smile.

"It's just—it's just ever since the robot thing, he's been acting really weird. Like, OK, I know this is going to sound dumb, but my dad never gets my name right on the first try. All of my brothers' and sisters' names begin with 'ch,' and he'll go through all of them when he calls me. 'Cheyenne, Charity, Christian, Charlie.' Every time. Sometimes he even adds the dog. But ever since the robot thing, he's called me by my name on the first try. He hasn't messed up once."

Charlie stopped to let that sink in. I looked around. "Uhhhh, so you think something's wrong with your dad because he knows your name?"

Charlie sighed. "I know it sounds stupid."

"Charlie, your dad was in hiding for two weeks," I said. "Aren't you just glad to have him back?"

"I don't know if I have him back," Charlie blurted out.

"Charlie . . . "

"I don't know if he's back. He does all this weird stuff, like he goes to bed at the same time every night. The EXACT same time right down to the second—10:47:32—even when I try to stall him! I've timed him with several different watches."

"Charlie . . . "

"And he keeps asking about you. Like all the time. And not like if you're doing OK, but he always wants to know what you've talked about. And then when I try to have a conversation with him, sometimes he'll stare ahead with a faraway look in his eye like he's not listening, but then he can perfectly recite every word I've said."

"Charlie . . . "

"But here's the big thing." Charlie looked both ways and pulled out a Frisbee-looking disk attached to a wire and plug. "I sneaked into my parents' bedroom and found this underneath the mattress. Do you know what it is?"

I sighed and shrugged. "What?"

"A wireless battery charger. Like for cell phones."

"Okayyyy . . . "

"But it's way too big for a phone. So I took it apart and looked up the manufacturer. The manufacturer is a new company in New Mexico that makes androids."

"An android is like a robot?"

"A very human-looking robot."

“So what are you saying?” I asked.

Charlie was already talking quietly, but he delivered the next two sentences in a whisper. “I don’t think that’s my dad at all. I think it’s a robot.”

About the Author

Dustin Brady

Dustin Brady lives in Cleveland, Ohio, with his wife, Deserae; dog, Nugget; and kids. He has spent a good chunk of his life getting crushed over and over in *Super Smash Bros.* by his brother Jesse and friend Eric. You can learn what he's working on next at dustinbradybooks.com and e-mail him at dustin@dustinbradybooks.com.

Jesse Brady

Jesse Brady is a professional illustrator and animator, who lives in Pensacola, Florida. His wife, April, is an awesome illustrator, too! When he was a kid, Jesse loved drawing pictures of his favorite video games, and he spent lots of time crushing his brother Dustin in *Super Smash Bros.* over and over again. You can see some of Jesse's best work at jessebradyart.com, and you can e-mail him at jessebradyart@gmail.com.

MORE TO EXPLORE

One of the first things you'll realize once you begin programming is that computers aren't smart, but they have great memories. For example, a computer could never figure out how to make a peanut butter and jelly sandwich on its own. But once you teach a computer how to make a PB&J, it'll never forget.

Because computers have such good memories, programmers use little shortcuts called **"functions"** to teach a job once and then repeat it over and over in their code.

The first time you want a computer to make a peanut butter and jelly sandwich, you'll need to teach it to get two slices of bread, spread peanut butter on one slice, spread jelly on the other slice, and then put the two slices together. However, if you want the computer to make lots of PB&Js in the future (and why wouldn't you?), you could just use a function to give that job a name—Peanut Butter and Jelly Sandwich. Now every time you type "Peanut Butter and Jelly Sandwich" into your code, the computer will remember how to build the sandwich and deliver a delicious lunch.

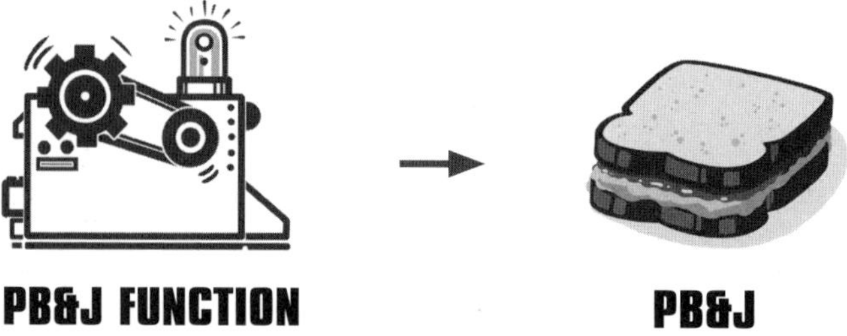

That's pretty cool, but what's even cooler is that you can train functions to do a bunch of different jobs. For example, instead of naming the function Peanut Butter and Jelly Sandwich, you could just name it Sandwich. This function could then make peanut butter and jelly sandwiches, as well as ham and cheese sandwiches, BLT sandwiches, and those gross grown-up sandwiches with olives and spicy mustard.

You'd build this tasty function by telling the computer that a sandwich is a list of ingredients smooshed between two slices of bread. Then you can swap out ingredients to build whatever sandwich you want. Programmers call these ingredients **"parameters."**

This book has a real-life function in it. Do you remember it? It's the walking robot factory Jesse sees in the sewer. The factory could assemble all kinds of robots—it just needed to know what parts to use.

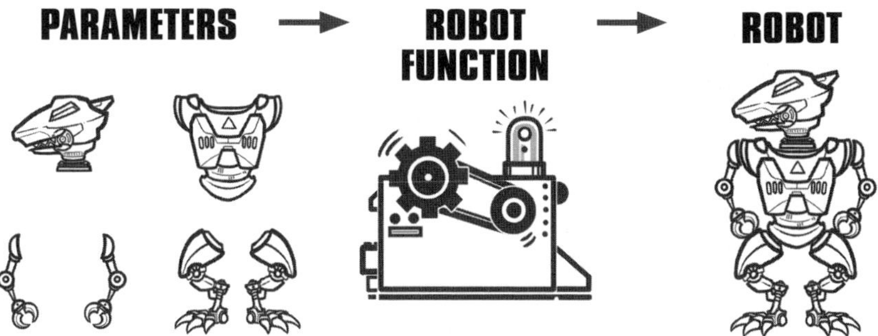

In this section, you'll use functions and parameters to build custom robots. Check out the robot parts over the next four pages, then use the functions on the last two pages to put them together.

Heads

SPACE DROID

CYBORG GENIUS

MECH SHARK

Torsos

EXPLORATION SUIT

BATTLE SUIT

SPEED SUIT

Arms

CLAW CONTROL

ROBO REVENGE

SAMURAI SLASHER

Legs

FUTURE KICKS

JURASSIC STEEL

SPIDEY SLICERS

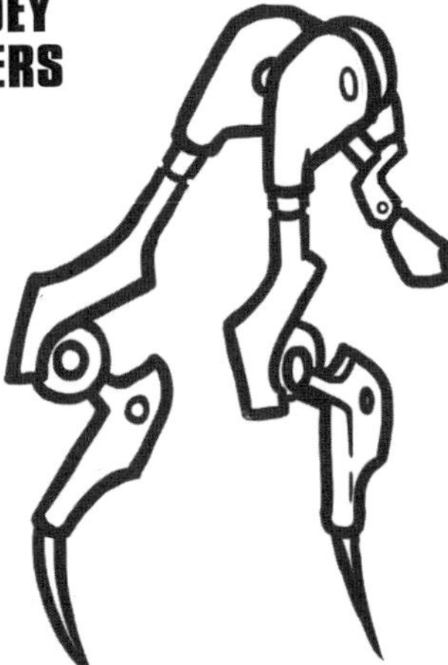

Robot Function Factory

Now for the fun part! In this exercise, you'll act as the robot function factory by assembling parts from the previous pages into complete robots. Simply draw or trace each robot part listed in the parameters below.

PARAMETERS → **ROBOT FUNCTION**

Mech Shark

Battle Suit

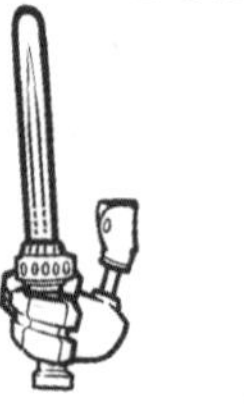

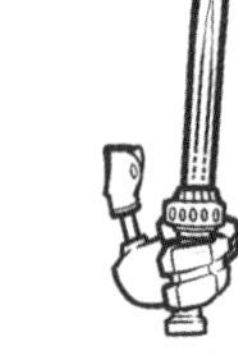

Samurai Slasher

Future Kicks

ROBOT

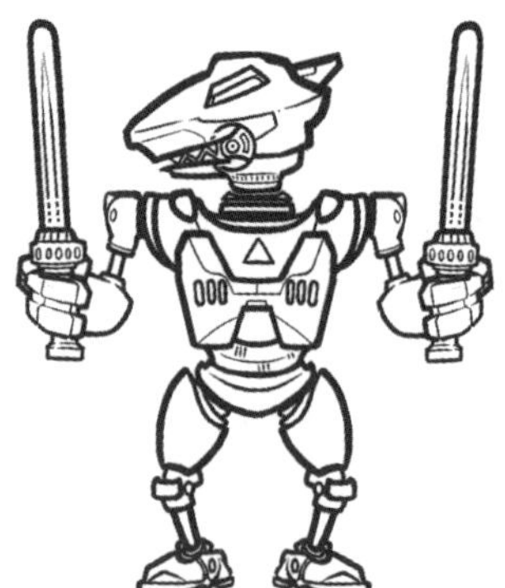

Great White Sea Pirate

PARAMETERS → **ROBOT FUNCTION** → **ROBOT**

Cyborg Genius

Speed Suit

Robo Revenge

Spidey Slicers

Tarantutron

PARAMETERS → **ROBOT FUNCTION** → **ROBOT**

Space Droid

Battle Suit

Claw Control

Jurassic Steel

Velocibot 3000

PARAMETERS → **ROBOT FUNCTION** → **ROBOT**

Mech Shark

Exploration Suit

Robo Revenge

Spidey Slicers

Deep-Sea Metal Monster

Look for these books!

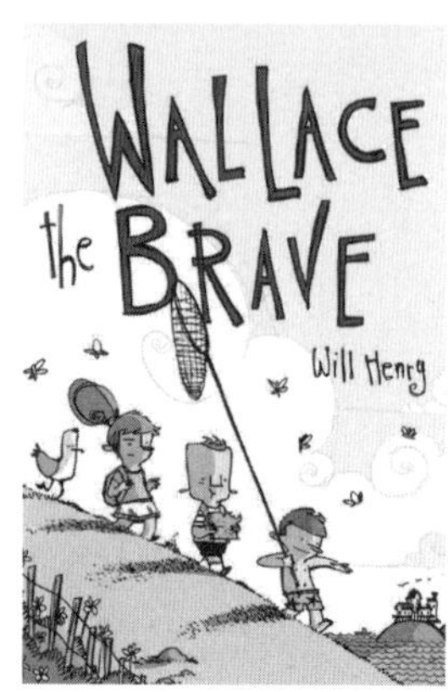